August Wilhelm Iffland

The Lawyers

A drama, in five acts

August Wilhelm Iffland

The Lawyers
A drama, in five acts

ISBN/EAN: 9783337394783

Printed in Europe, USA, Canada, Australia, Japan

Cover: Foto ©Andreas Hilbeck / pixelio.de

More available books at **www.hansebooks.com**

THE

LAWYERS,

A

DRAMA,

IN FIVE ACTS,

TRANSLATED

FROM THE GERMAN

OF

Augustus William Iffland.

BY C. LUDGER.

London:

PRINTED BY J. W. MYERS,

FOR W. WEST, NO. 27, PATERNOSTER-ROW.

1799.

[*Price Two Shillings and Sixpence.*]

ADVERTISEMENT.

———

THE Author of the following Drama is universally allowed to be the Garrick of the German Stage, and the Dramatic Rival of KOTZEBUE in the Closet.—The great Object of MR. IFFLAND, in all his Dramatic Productions, is to render the Theatre what it was in the palmy Days of Terence—a School of Morality, by exhibiting Virtue in all her native Charms, and Vice in all her Deformity; or, in the Language of Pope,

" To wake the Soul by gentle Strokes of Art,
" To raise the Genius, and to mend the Heart;
" In conscious Innocence to make Men bold,
" Live o'er each Scene, and be what you behold!"

DRAMATIS PERSONÆ.

———

Deputy CLARENBACH.
CLARENBACH, Master Carpenter.
FREDERICA, his Daughter.
REISSMAN, Aulic Counsellor.
SOPHIA, his Daughter.
SELLING, Counsellor.
GERNAU, Ranger.
WELLENBERG, Lawyer.
GROBMAN, Iron Merchant.
LEWIS, Deputy Clarenbach's Servant.
A Servant of the Aulic Counsellor.

LAWYERS,

^

DRAMA.

ACT I.

SCENE I.

*A plain Tradesman's Room, with old fashioned
Furniture.*

Master CLARENBACH. *(Busied with a design.)*

Clar. SO!—there is my design, and I think
it is a pretty good one. It will
make a substantial building.—When I am
gone, people will say, when they look at the
pile, " Master Clarenbach was a man that
knew what he was about."

SCENE II.

Enter LEWIS.

Lew. Deputy Clarenbach presents his com-
liments to Master Clarenbach, and sends him
fomething.

Clar. What?

Lew. Deputy Clarenbach presents his compliments, and sends something.

B

Clar. *(takes off his spectacles.)* So my son sends me his compliments? So! well,—return him a good morrow from me. What is it he sends?—money! *(opens the paper;)* for what? he has written nothing in it, a mere blank.

Lew. I do not know; I am to have a receipt for it.

Clar. Take the money back.

Lew. What the deuce!

Clar. *(rises.)* No deuce here! and—take off your hat when you stand in my presence, Monsieur Lewis.

Lew. *(takes off his hat reluctantly.)* I am—

Clar. The Deputy's footman, and I am the Deputy's father.

Lew. Aye, aye; Master Clarenbach, the—

Clar. The carpenter, citizen and master, trustee of the hospital, *ad Sanctum Mauritium* in this town, master in my own house and in my own room; here is the money. I am busy, good bye. *(Sits down to his design.)*

Lew. Very odd.   [*Exit.*

Clar. Odd? hem! aye, aye. Odd you are, both the master and the servant.

SCENE III.

Enter FREDERICA, *(with a glass of wine, and a crust of bread on a plate.)*

Fred. Father, the weather is very rough this morning.

Clar. Do you think so, my dear?

Fred. I cannot let you go out of the house so; you must take a glass of wine.

Clar. You are right, I think; *(takes it.)* Moreover, I fhall be out a good while to day; *(drinks;)* perhaps I may not come home to dinner; *(drinks;)* bring my dinner then to the timber-yard.

Fred. With all my heart.

Clar. (looking at her.) I do not think you will do it with reluctance.

Fred. By no means. I will do it with pleasure. But my brother does not altogether relifh it; and, in those little matters, I think we might please him.

Clar. (rises displeased.) I say, no! God bless him in the high station he fills! But that cannot be, if ever he fhould forget what he has been. And as his memory, in that respect, is daily impaired, it is necessary therefore to put him the oftener in mind of it.

Fred. Yet I think—

Clar. He is a Deputy,—let him thank God for it! I am a carpenter, thank heaven! You are my good dutiful daughter, that takes care of me, nurses me, and gives me great satisfaction; and for that, I return heaven threefold thanks from the bottom of my heart. *(Fred. embraces him.)* Yes, you are very good! I only find fault with two things; in every other respect you are a nice girl, quite the girl after my own heart. First, you read too much, and then—

Fred. Dear father, do not I tell you a number of entertaining and instructive things out of the books I read? Has my reading formed me otherwise than you would have me?

Clar. Not as yet, if the evil do not come limping at the end! Good God!—Books indeed impart information; that I must own. But since those deep learned works have carried thy brother so high, and, at the same time, so far from us; I think, when I behold the large heap of books in his study, I think I see a finger-post that directs from the heart.

Fred. Your pursuits and his are different, father.

Clar. In our respective lines, I grant it. If his heart were not a stranger to us from other motives, he would, when his work is done, come and say,—Father! you build houses, and I build laws, that the people may live secure in those houses. I have been successful to day in my work, if God should prosper it; and how have you succeeded? Then I would talk to him of my good old timber, and complain of the young green wood; he might then tell me, how pleased he is with the old colleagues that share his toils, or complain of the young green ones.—Thus we might exchange toil and pleasure, complaint and consolation; spend a comfortable hour together, and derive mutual advantage from each other. But he does not choose to do that; and, if his conscience now and then happen to twitch him a little, he sends me money. Money! what is money to me? when have I ever wished for more than to live? *(With vivacity.)* His money is the only thing I dislike about him.

Fred. Why so, father?

Clar. Because he has not that great quantity of it—hem! there—there, may be enough of it for this time. The second thing I do not like in you is to see you converse with that Counsellor Selling. What is the meaning of it?

Fred. My brother entertains a high esteem for him.

Clar. Not I.

Fred. He is pleased to see him visit here.

Clar. Not I. And then have you not Gernau, the Ranger, whom you like, and I too?

Fred. Well, are you content if I manage so, that I may keep upon good terms with both?

Clar. I have no objection. But mind, all fair! none of your book stories! *(Looks at his watch.)* Half past eleven; you will bring my dinner to the yard.

Fred. Undoubtedly. [*Exit.*

SCENE IV.

Enter REISSMAN.

Reiss. Aye, good morrow, Miss! Good morrow, Mr. Clarenbach! Well, how are you?

Clar. At work, Sir!

Reiss. So you have, *ex officio,* been appointed guardian of the poor orphans of Brunnig?

Clar. Yes, Sir, these four days.

Reiss. Aye, aye; it will prove a troublesome piece of business. Poor children! I pity them.

Clar. So do I.—And, to tell you the truth, the valuable bequest of the old aunt ought to go to the children, and not to you; to whom, contrary to all right and equity, she has bequeathed her all.

Reiss. Aye! Good heaven!—but then it is so in her will.

Clar. True enough. But the law should not permit it.

Reiss. A last will!—O Lord! that is a sacred thing. I pity the children, but—

Clar. I intend to try the validity of it.

Reiss. Aye, aye? I have been told so.

Clar. You ought to decline the bequest, Mr, Reissman.

Reiss. But, what heaven has sent me—

Clar. The property of orphans!

Reiss. You would not have me rob my child of the divine blessings which, without the least solicitation on my part, have devolved upon me from a strange person?

Clar. Your daughter is not poor. The children of Brunnig are all beggars.

Reiss. Aye, good man, we will manage that, we will manage it!

Clar. How so?

Reiss. O heaven! Yes, we will send the children to the hospital to receive a christian education, and to be instructed, and I will—

Clar. To what hospital?

Reiss. To ours, of which I am the director, and you a trustee.

Clar. That will not do.

Reiss. If it be our will—

Clar. It must not be our will.

Reiss. Who is to oppose us?

Clar. The rules of the foundation itself; right and equity. The hospital, *ad Sanctum Mauritium*, is destined for the old and the sick; we must not displace them. No, I will carry on the suit against you as an unlawful heir.—

Reiss. Aye, thou good Lord in heaven! the will is so plain—

Clar. If I am cast, I will take Brunnig's children into my house, and then I will immediately engage in more business, employ more hands, and work hard to accomplish my design, with the aid of heaven.

Reiss. But your son, the deputy, approves of the children being sent to the hospital.

Clar. I do not approve of it.

Reiss. Your son is a sensible learned man, who most certainly knows—

Clar. And I have spent a good deal on him too.

Reiss. And a just man too he is.

Clar. That is his duty.

Reiss. And as these children may be taken care of in another manner, why would you, at your time of life, burthen yourself with more trouble? You have now toiled long enough, and to your credit too: now you should rest, and leave off business.

Clar. God forbid!

Reiss. Your son will not give up that point, I tell you: as a good son, he will lead his father to honour.

Clar. To honour? And what honour do I want, pray? I am a good workman, have sufficient to live on, employ fifteen people daily; share my earnings with many a poor man, and have a good conscience. What honour can he add to what I have?

Reiss. This very moment it is in agitation, to elect you mayor of our town. That is as good as settled, only—

Clar. No, Sir! I will not listen to that. I am quite well, when governed; and might not be so, if I were to govern others.

Reiss. But consider, how happy many a man would feel, if he—

Clar. Oh yes! I know well enough: many a man would wish to govern now-a-days; but not L: I intend to remain reigning master-carpenter in my own house and timber-yard.

Reiss. But perhaps your son might form connections—

Clar. A fig for every connection; cannot he form connections unless his father be mayor?

Reiss. The world has its prejudices—

Clar. Not I.

Reiss. To whom it is often prudent to yield.

Clar. No, Sir, no!

Reiss. But, suppose your son should wish to rise still higher?

Clar. Then God grant it do him good! that is my cordial wish. But I shall remain where I am, and I shall not climb after him.

Reiss. Well then, I must speak plain to you; your son pays his addresses to my daughter.

Clar. Does he? that is well done. Your daughter is an amiable young lady.

Reiss. Well, well;—but then I have some conditions to propose. I only desire that you may change your situation in life.

Clar. Does your daughter likewise insist on it?

Reiss. Suppose she did?

Clar. Then I would, were I in my son's place, decline the hand of a lady that would be ashamed of my father.

Reiss. But, if I should only ask that you shall leave off business—

Clar. Leave off business? I might as well leave off living. I am proud of my business, for, upon my word, I am a good carpenter.

Reiss. Well then, you may say you have been a carpenter. When you are Mayor, I will, with pleasure, call you brother. Only accept the office, and we will see the business taken care of.

Clar. No. I would be what I was called. I had better keep away from your council-board.

Reiss. I have now done my duty. Consider, that when the children come out of the hospital, I intend to make them a present. And that, if an action is brought against me, I shall not think myself under any obligation whatever.

Clar. Do not take it amiss;—I am rather positive, for I am arrived at the age in which people know which way the world turns, be-

c

cause they have often been forced to turn along with it. Should the poor children lose their suit, you are not the man neither of whom I should wish them take alms.

Reiss. Oh! if matters stand so, then I will do nothing at all, for my conscience is free, thank God.

Clar. I wish you joy.

Reiss. As for the rest, it is now all in your option, whether you will promote your son's happiness through that marriage, or not. I wish you good business, Master Clarenbach.

Clar. (alone.) Hem, hem!—I do not wish it, I know well enough;—but I should be sorry for Jack, if he were to lose the girl on that account.

SCENE V.

Enter GROBMAN.

Grob. Your humble servant, Mr. Clarenbach.

Clar. Servant, Sir! What is your pleasure?

Grob. My name is Grobman. I deal in iron wholesale.

Clar. Well; and—

Grob. And mean to settle here.

Clar. I wish you success.

Grob. But there is an other, who wishes to do the same,—one Benninger.

Clar. Success to him likewise!

Grob. He is for having the monopoly of the article here.

Clar. If so, I look upon him in a bad point of view.

Grob. But it is very profitable. I have the same object in view. Your son, the deputy, patronizes Mr. Benninger. But, if you would speak in my favour to your son, I know I should succeed.

Clar. I am a carpenter.

Grob. Very right. But then you are the Deputy's father. Benninger, as I am well informed, has secretly offered your son two thousand dollars by way of present.

Clar. What?

Grob. They have agreed.

Clar. Infamous calumny!

Grob. I will give you two hundred dollars beside, if you—

Clar. Set off!—for, upon my word, I will do you some mischief.

Grob. Do you want more than two hundred?

Clar. Justice I want, Justice! My son shall send you to prison, unless he be as great a good for nothing as yourself.

Grob. (*laughs.*) For what?

Clar, Sell! sell a monopoly! take money,— a bribe! My son, Jack Clarenbach, the sovereign's deputy, take money!

Grob. (*laughs.*) Aye, sure, for the trouble that he—

Clar. I will bring an action against you.

Grob. Are you in your senses?

Clar. I will inform—

Grob. So you may.

Clar. All you have said.

Grob. Do so.

Clar. My son shall have ample satisfaction, Where is your conscience, fellow? Defame a man in office and dignity? Now, go out by that door, or I will lay both my hands on you.

Grob. The man must be tipsy. *(Laughs, and exit.)*

Clar. Aye, you may laugh, you cursed thief, All my limbs tremble!—Some envious man, some fiend has sent him hither.—Jack would not betray his native town,

SCENE VI.

Enter FREDERICA,

Clar. It is not possible.

Fred. Only think, dear father—

Clar. Curse the money!

Fred. Brother Jack is—

Clar. He has too much. Yes, yes, yes! I know, he has too much, and it is impossible that he acquired it all in a fair way; but not so neither. It may have been scraped together somewhat unfairly; but not so neither, not so neither.

Fred. What ails you, pray? What do you talk about Jack and his money?

Clar. I cannot bear it, cannot bear his money.

Fred. Only think; Ranger Gernau sends me word, that yesterday the news arrived, that my brother has been made a Privy Counsellor.

Clar. Privy Counsellor ?—hem !—Curse that iron merchant, that—

Fred. He is now the first man in this town.

Clar. Take money! sell privileges! *(walks up and down.)* It is impossible ! Father and mother are honest people; he has been sent to church and school, never saw any thing amiss in us; no, nothing amiss in all his life-time. We have worked hard day after day; never indulged ourselves with breakfast or bagging,* that he might have every requisite, that we might spend on him as much as ever we could afford. And now, he is got up so high, and is one of those that rule the country, that now he should be worse than I would suffer a 'prentice boy to be, that I employ in my yard! Oh! if that be so, Lord take him or me, for I cannot bear it, either in this world or in the next!   [*Exit.*

Fred. I do not understand a word of all this. What does he mean?

SCENE VII.

Enter GERNAU.

Gern. Good morrow, Frederica!

---

* *Bagging,* in the North of England, is the common expression for a meal taken between dinner and supper. And, as it perfectly expresses the meaning of the German *vesperbrod,* I thought myself authorized to adopt it here; particularly as *tea,* in the mouth of a character, like carpenter Clarenbach, would appear preposterous. The antiquaries of Yorkshire and Lancashire derive the word *bagging* from the old custom of carrying bread and cheese in a bag, in the afternoon, to the labourers in the fields; and this derivation is not altogether improbable.

                                              Translator.

Fred. Why so ruffled? Is that your welcome, after having kept out of the way for two
days together?

Gern. Things grow worse and worse, between your brother and me, every day.

Fred. Why so?

Gern. He would have me do things which I
neither can, must, nor will do.

SCENE VIII.

Enter CLARENBACH,

Clar. Jack a Privy Counsellor, you say?

Fred. Gernau says so,

Gern. His diploma arrived yesterday.

Clar. He has not mentioned it to me.

Fred. He will most certainly come to day,

Clar. But could he wait till to day?

Fred. Who knows but he wishes to surprise us?

Clar. He is going to be married too,

Fred. My brother?

Clar. I am told all this by strangers. Can
he turn out so, because he is a greater man
than I? or, perhaps, he is altogether bad,—
God knows!

Fred. He is so full of business.

Clar. So am I.

Fred. Those that work with the head are
apt to be more absent than those that work
with the hand.

Clar. But is it not a real relaxation to act
according to the dictates of the heart? or have
the hearts of those people nothing to do with

their concerns? If so, they are wretched be-
ings indeed, and I am very sorry for my son,
that he must first lose the treasures of his heart
to hoard up gold. [*Exit.*

SCENE IX.

FREDERICA, GERNAU.

Fred. Tell me immediately, dear Gernau,
what is the matter between you and my brother?

Gern. He is not a good man, Frederica.

Fred. Shall I go to him, Gernau?

Gern. Do not embitter my life, good soul;
I have trouble enough besides. Your brother
will drive me away.

Fred. What?

Gern. He will throw me out of my office.

Fred. Why?

Gern. To put a more accommodating man
in my place.

Fred. He does not wish to do that certainly,
nor could he even effect it.

Gern. He is all-powerful here; his abilities,
his connections at Court, his office, render
every thing possible that he wishes to atchieve.

Fred. And what does he want of you? what
displeases him?

Gern. Under the pretence of promoting agri-
culture, he wants the best part of the forest for
himself, which is of no great use to the commu-
nity. And this pretended plea is a garden, he
means to lay out in the English style for his
own pleasure.

Fred. And should not an industrious man be indulged with some pleasure?

Gern. Should he wish to have it at the expence of the public? I must oppose it.

Fred. Does he know it?

Gern. Yes, he behaved so haughtily to me.

Fred. And you—

Gern. I thought on his sister,—and held my tongue.

Fred. (reaches him her hand.) Gernau!

Gern. He threatened me!

Fred. And you?

Gern. I curbed my passion. He bid me be gone,—and I shall not trouble him again.

Fred. And what do you intend to do as to the forest?

Gern. My duty.

Fred. (draws back her hand.) Oh!

Gern. Yes, yes! It will cost me your hand, I foresee.

Fred. Never!—my affection is fixed, and can never be diverted from the dear object.—Your complaisance—

Gern. I have been complaisant, as far as laid in my power. I cannot be so at the expence of my duty.

Fred. I do not insist on that either. But,—but—

Gern. What would you wish that your own sentiments of equity forbids you to utter?

Fred. I only wish—I demand nothing—I only wish you to soften your rigid idea of duty, if you can.

Gern. I know nothing but justice, that will not admit of any by-road. And if I were capable of such a sacrifice, whither would it lead me? It would lead me to see you, Selling's wife, and to laugh at me.

Fred. Must I break with all the world, because our hearts beat in unison? Am I criminal to listen to Selling's nonsense, because he is the only man through whom I can act upon my brother?

Gern. Then I may rely upon you?

Fred. Undoubtedly.

Gern. Pledge me your hand!

Fred. With all my heart!

Gern. Thus love will not forsake me, when I shall fall a victim to my duty.

Fred. I know no deceit, and follow the dictates of my heart.

Gern. In the name of heaven then I go to discharge my duty; it rewards and strengthens. Good bye, Frederica!—One more word, you are good; but are you resolute?

Fred. I am indeed!

Gern. Your brother has plans about you, in which I am most certainly set down for nought. —Frederica, Frederica, let him drive me hence, but not from you!

Fred. He shall not, he cannot. And no man can render me inconstant to you, but yourself.

Gern. Then you are mine, and I am easy.

Fred. And owe no grudge to my brother?

Gern. Frederica, I am an honest man.

D

Fred. Whom the purest love shall reward, as far as love can reward!

Gern. Adieu, dear Frederica!

Fred. Adieu, Gernau!

[*Exeunt by opposite doors.*

ACT II.

SCENE I.

A room in the Privy Counsellor's, furnished in the modern stile.

REISSMAN, LEWIS.

Lew. I shall have the honour to let the Privy Counsellor know, that the Aulic Counsellor Reissman waits. (*Steps into a closet, out of which the Privy Counsellor immediately comes, and Lewis sometime after.*)

Reiss. I fly to congratulate you on your well-merited elevation.

P. Coun. I thank you with all my heart. I shall never forget that I am indebted to you for it.

Reiss. I beg,—nay, I entreat—

P. Coun. Your advice.

Reiss. Too much modesty.

P. Coun. Your self-denial. For you yourself had the justest claims to all the honours, with which you permitted me to be invested.

Reiss. Audaces fortuna.—I am too old. Now you should enjoy life, my friend. The merchant will endeavour to get a hundred per cent. if he can; why should the statesman sell his labour to the state at three? Away with the silly prejudice, and the retail-trade of your conscientious precepts; carry on your business wholesale, on the sacred principle of self-preservation.

P. Coun. I partly do so, but my father—

Reiss. I have paid the old honest man a visit.

P. Coun. Very kind of you! very kind of you indeed!

Reiss. He persists in his determination of setting the will aside.

P. Coun. Ridiculous!

Reiss. He will not suffer the children to go to the hospital, because the institution is intended for old and decayed people.

P. Coun. Mere formalities, attached to old age!

Reiss. As for the rest, he appeared pleased with your proposed union with my daughter.

P. Coun. Was he!

Reiss. He said many handsome things of the girl.

P. Coun. Too much cannot be said in her praise. She is an angel.

Reiss. I humbly thank you.—But he will not accept the office of mayor on any account.

P. Coun. I thought so;—but he must.

Reiss. Oh, yes! I must request you to carry that point, for—

P. Coun. Without doubt.

Reiss. For, however pleased I may be with your connection, I could not possibly think of giving my daughter to a man whose father earned his bread as a mechanic.

P. Coun. Leave me alone for that. His whole mode of life will be changed. Nay, this change has in some measure taken place already.

Reiss. Bravo, bravo!

P. Coun. His mansion—

Reiss. Right, right!

P. Coun. His dress—

Reiss. Very necessary.

P. Coun. Those pitiful caps of my sister—

Reiss. Oh, nice! Oh! there you remove a heavy weight from my mind. And then the chief object, that law-suit—

P. Coun. You cannot lose it. The will—

Reiss. I will stick to that, as if rivetted to it with iron.

P. Coun. It speaks in your favour in all its forms.

Reiss. But he is so obstinate in pursuit of the cause, and will—

P. Coun. He cannot gain it.

Reiss. I think so. But then he has engaged that old foolish lawyer Wellenberg, that—

P. Coun. A fool, and a pedant.

Reiss. True! But then he is such a conscientious fellow; and, besides, you know he is called the champion of the poor and the guardian of orphans.

P. Coun. I have his opinion in my study.
Mere declamation! nothing else. Your answer
is sound, legal, and argumentative, and then
the testamentary disposition is so plain that it
cannot be set aside. If you were inclined to
make the plaintiff a present—

Reiss. O yes, O yes! notwithstanding I am
very economical; for all that I acquire is solely
intended for my child, and when it shall please
heaven to call me, it will devolve to you, my
dear Sir.

P. Coun. Very kind;—but—

Enter LEWIS.

Lew. The widow Rieder—

P. Coun. Some other time.

Lew. And Counsellor Wellenberg—

P. Coun. The day after to-morrow, at two
o'clock.

Lew. Then there is old Schwartz—

P. Coun. I cannot be troubled with him
now.   [*Exit Lewis.*

Reiss. Always plagued, always tormented.—

P. Coun. Oh! there is no end of it!

Reiss. Why! But wealth and honours
are very welcome things too. But chiefly
mind wealth; wealth is the word. High sta-
tions are exposed to storms, like lofty trees
in a forest. But, if you have wealth, then
come what will. A trunk filled with good
bonds is soon packed up. The rest of your
moveables may be left to the commissaries, just

as you would throw a few bones to the dogs;
then retire and go. I am your servant. *(Going.)*

[*Privy Counsellor attends him to the door.*

Reiss. No ceremony; the morning-hour
yields a hundred per cent. [*Exit.*

SCENE II.

PRIVY COUNSELLOR, LEWIS, MASTER
CLARENBACH,·

Lew. I will first see.

Clar. Why, I heard my son's voice!—

P. Coun. Ah! is it my father?—

Clar. Yes! *(reaches him his hand.)* God bless
you, Jack!

P. Coun. *(to Lewis.)* Leave us to ourselves.

[*Lewis exit,*

Clar. Halloo!—I say, Monsieur, stop a
little, stay a little!—I mean to speak ill of you.

Lew. So?

P. Coun. How so?

Clar. Only think, dear Jack, all the people
you have refused to see, this fellow has been
snarling at. *(To Lewis.)* You must know
those people in the hall are all as good as myself, and my son has been what I am, and in
short we are all—men. Whilst the people
know that my son has not forgot that his rank
and titles are pure gold, they will pass at the
highest course of exchange; but, as soon as they
discover he has forgot what he has been, then
his rank and titles will appear counterfeit.
(To the Privy Counsellor.) They are all in the
hall yet, except the old lawyer, who has busi-

ness elsewhere; I have told them Monsieur
Lewis had behaved very unmannerly, that I
would let you know, and that you would come
out to them.

P. Coun. But—

Clar. And that you may remain in currency
and value, be so good, Jack, and go to them.

[*Privy Coun. after a pause, leaves the room.*

SCENE III.

MASTER CLARENBACH, LEWIS.

Lew. I do not understand Master Clarenbach's behaviour to me.

Clar. I dare say, you do not. But, do you
see, I think you ought to mend, or my son
ought to send you about your business. To
hear people, to say either yes or no, is the
least my son can do. If you should attempt to
hinder him from doing so, you are a rogue.

Lew. There is such constant intrusion.

Clar. Hem! and a great deal of distress too,
and—   [*Exit Lewis.*

SCENE IV.

Enter PRIVY COUNSELLOR.

P. Coun. Well, what should it be? Petitions, memorials, poverty, and faint hopes of
relief.

Clar. Why, if you cannot relieve, mercy on
us!

P. Coun. They are repeated so often, and
I have so much business—

Clar. Now that you have been made a Privy

Counsellor, I fear it will still be worse! Well, heaven grant you health, and may you act as you ought, and all may be well yet.

P. Coun. Why, father, did you return the money 1 sent?—

Clar. Because, thank God! I do not want it. What is the use of having more than is necessary, to supply the wants of life?—1 think you have more.

P. Coun. There is no great harm in that.

Clar. But I think there is! People will have strange ideas, and do strange things, when they have too much. If I must tell you my mind, son, I am not altogether pleased to see you raised so high of a sudden, Our plain citizens are not altogether satisfied with you and your elevation. They think the other gentlemen shove you near the fire to get the roasted chesnuts out of the coals for themselves, and that you are a good cat's paw. Such, for instance, is that bequest to old Counsellor Reissman.

P. Coun. Pray, tell me, father, what induces you to oppose that will, which is legal, though 1 must own it bears hard on the children.

Clar. Jack, you know your father long, though for some time since you have made a stranger of yourself.—What would you think of me, if 1 had not commenced the suit?

P. Coun. The claim rests on a will.

Clar. Which has been obtained, by the old Counsellor, by undue influence; is not that your opinion?

P. Coun. Can that be proved?—

Clar. We must see—

P. Coun. If you cannot prove it, the Coun-sellor will recover.

Clar. He certainly will, and therefore you must assist me to combat him.

P. Coun. Who, I? How came you to think so? Well, we will leave the cause to take its due course, and so should you.—

Clar. Ay, ay, Jack.

P. Coun. Besides, I must tell you, Reiss-man proposes to give me his daughter.

Clar. So I hear. The lady has all my best wishes. Heaven prosper your union! But sure you would not begin it by an act of in-justice!

P. Coun. No, certainly not! But why would you, suppose even though Reissman were wrong,—why would you, for the sake of strangers, destroy my happiness?

Clar. Can poor, injured, unhappy children, in any situation, be *strangers* to me? And have wards, intrusted to my care, fewer titles to my assistance than my own children? And have not you, in the name of the ma-gistrates, appointed me one of their guar-dians?

P. Coun. That, as they are unfortunate, I might see them in good hands.

Clar. Why, they are in good hands. I am come to request you to see the business speedily executed. Of the verdict itself I will make no mention. You will act as an honest man, or else I must despise you, and look for redress elsewhere. Meanwhile, I tell you, the children shall not go to the hospital, because that is impracticable.

P. Coun. Father, I have given my word.

Clar. You must recall it.

P. Coun. How can I?

Clar. Say you did not understand the matter. It is upon my word better than to expose your name to shame or ridicule, and to fill your mind with inquietude.

P. Coun. Father, I love you dearly, but pray do not interfere with my business.

Clar. Very well; then you act as Privy Counsellor, as you think proper; and I, as trustee of the hospital and guardian of the children, will do the same.

P. Coun. Cannot we talk of more agreeable things, and drop that question. I wish you so well, but you reject all I propose.

Clar. You make me presents in money, and, I am told, you want to make me mayor of the town. Jack, make me no presents! do good to town and country; and, if you can, come after your business is done. I do not care if it be but once or twice every three months; come to me in my timber-yard. Then we will close the doors, seat ourselves in the little bower, where, when a boy, you used to sit so industriously about your tasks; there we will spend an hour in happy converse, and drink a glass of old wine that you shall send me; then I will thank God for my dear boy, who has continued to be a good son, and, when you leave me again to repair to your desk, I will give you my blessing, and look after you, till you are quite out of sight! Do you see, Jack, I ask no more;—I have no occasion for more; but this I earnestly request of you. Give me your hand, that you will do it. That is the way I wish you to honour and to please me.

P. Coun. I shall do more, father. Pray accept it, and—

Clar. All your other honours are of little estimation in my sight; thefe grey hairs, blanched with care and toil, shall never be covered with a long bushy wig; look at these hands, rough with labour; look on your father, as you know his ways; you also know that he is neither to be drawn nor driven out of them; Master Claronbach, even in the office of Mayor, would not suit your fine apartments and your fine company. What, to remain at home, as motionless as an old statue, scarce permitted to speak to an old friend, lest it should lessen his dignity, or break in on his gravity! What, to remain in such a situation, and see people work and move before his window! Jack, that will not do. Pray, as I never found fault with you for being too high, do not find fault with me for being too low; it is best suited to my age and inclinations.

P. Coun. Certainly not; but Mr. Reissman insists on it, as a principal condition.

Clar. I hope you know that there is a wide difference betwixt your father and Mr. Reissman. My axe, since I could raise it, has been employed in raising houses for the industrious, and his pen, since he could handle it, in pulling them down again.

P. Coun. This is the only service you can render me now father ; is it not unkind to re-fufe me then ?

Clar. The only service I can render you now ? What, if the cares and inquietudes of rank and office should lay you on a sick bed, who would attend you with so much tenderness and affection as your old father? What if your house should take fire, I would be the first to ascend through the flames ; but I will not climb into office and rank, I tell you that.

P. Coun. You must give way, father.—

Clar. You now stand on high ; may you so stand respected by your fellow citizens and approved by your own conscience is the sincerest wish of your old father! There-fore, I prefer my complaints to you against a man ; his name is Grobman, an ironmonger. This wretch wanted to persuade me, that you had taken two thousand dollars from another, to let him have the monopoly. He offered me two hundred dollars, if I would gain you over to his interest. Arrest the vile slanderer.

P. Coun. That fellow is an ideot.

Clar. God forbid! he is much worse. I have told him I would inform against him, and so I have to a few of my acquaintances.

P. Coun. Why so?

Clar. That you should make an example of him.

P. Coun. What is all this fuss? Why do you interfere with·my concerns?

Clar. Concerns? I am as anxious for your honour as I am for your life! Do not you bear my name, which has always been as good as the best bond, in this place, time out of mind? Are not you my son? Are not you the representative of our sovereign? Is not the least stain visible on your ermine? Is it, or is it not true, Jack?—No, no, I say; it is impossible, it cannot be true!

P. Coun. It is possible; it is so, but done in a manner which cannot—

Clar. Do not speak, I will not know it. I—I—cannot *(going from him)* look on you. Is that your wisdom! your honour! your integrity! Have I, therefore,—well,—if matters are so with you, then do as you like; enquire no more after me, come no more to see me; you ought to be ashamed of yourself, in the presence of your honest father. Farewell, Jack; repent and amend. I will visit you no more, till you have altered your ways, and divided your cursed mammon among the poor. Live on your honest earnings; then come to me, tender me a clean hand, and I will bless you. *(Exit.)*

SCENE V.

PRIVY COUNSELLOR, *(alone.)*

P. Coun. Whimsical, honest man!—Whoever is forced up to the giddy summit, must
hold as fast as he can, and by what he can.

SCENE IV.

Enter Counsellor SELLING.

P. Coun. What part of the world have you
come from Selling?

Sell. From Miss Frederica.

P. Coun. From my sister? how is she? Has
the new furniture been carried home?

Sell. Beautiful, splendid! thanks to your
care! Old papa will open all his eyes when he
comes home. All the old furniture has been
carried off, and the room looks very elegant
with all the new things you have sent.

P. Coun. And Frederica?—

Sell. She was so uneasy, she did not know
what to do with herself. She fixed her eyes
on every article as it was carried off, as if she
took leave of an old friend. But the large
easy chair still remains; she grasped it with
both hands, and would not suffer it to be removed.

P. Coun. These people must be metamor-
phosed; we must see how they reconcile themselves to it.

Sel. But, what a man you are! What a noble heart, to be thus attached to your family!

P. Coun. Very natural. I am indebted to my father for so many things;—and Frederica is a good-natured creature.

Sell. More than that. I know none of her sex that strives so anxiously to cultivate her understanding, and to exalt her faculties to an extraordinary height.

P. Coun. (*gives him his hand.*) I am glad you find her so.

Sell. With your permission, Frederica will now assume a different dress, better suited to the furniture you have sent.

- *P. Coun.* I have to thank you for this attention.

Sell. By your direction I do all that lies in my power to fan the girl's ambition. If that Mr. Gernau only—

P. Coun. That fool! He shall be removed. All has been prepared, and is now determined on. He goes to Friethal. His patent is in hand.

Sell. It is too lenient for his stubborn opposition. This indulgence on your side will gain you every heart.

P. Coun. Do you think I am rather popular?

Sell. Popular? People venerate you with enthusiasm! And what have you not done to acquire this popularity? The formation of the new roads, under your wise regulation, with-

out any burthen to the individual ! the increase
of commerce—

  P. Coun. I have done a great deal ; I think
I may claim some merit.

  Sell. The abolition of beggary ; the institution for the support of the indigent—

  P. Coun. Oh ! there are so many things to
be done yet!

  Sell. And you have so much power in your
hand. What do you say to my last performance ?

  P. Coun. I have perused it. To be candid, you must apply yourself more to solid
knowledge. There are glaring faults in it.—

  Sell. Under your inspection—

  P. Coun. With all my heart. But you must
do more, and then the faults in orthography
are too numerous. Call in the assistance of
a good grammarian.

  Sell. I will endeavour—

  P. Coun. Your motion in the court-house
of yesterday, that the foot-passenger should
be prohibited to walk in the middle of the
street, has provoked some laughter.

  Sell. I wanted to propose something in my
turn too.

  P. Coun. It is too trifling. Wait for the
motions of the senior barristers, and—

  Sell. I wanted to give myself a little air of
consequence by a motion of my own, hence—

  P. Coun. No, no. If you have nothing of
greater consequence to propose, you had better
walk like the rest in the middle of the street.
(*They retire to the closet.*)

SCENE VII.

Master CLARENBACH'S *house.*

Instead of the furniture which appeared in the first act, a modern writing-desk and handsome chairs.

Enter FREDERICA, *followed by a servant with a large band-box.*

Fred. My name is Frederica; what do you want with me?

Serv. To take these things, madam.

Fred. I will take nothing.

Serv. And I will take back nothing.

Fred. Who has sent you to me?

Serv. Somebody that has a right, I suppose. *(Puts down the band-box, and retires.)*

Fred. (alone.) It may remain there, I will not touch it: I will not look at it. *(Going from the band-box.)* Sure, there are some articles of dress for me in it. It is odd that they will not leave us as we wish, to our own wishes. *(Draws a step nearer.)* It may not be for me perhaps. *(Reads the direction at a distance.)* To Miss Frederica Clarenbach; but it is addressed to me, I see! If any person,—if Gernau should happen to come in, I must remove the box. *(Takes hold of it.)* Quite light! as light as a feather! What does it contain? What is that to me? *(Takes it up, and walks a few paces.)* If Gernau should now meet me, it would look as if I wanted to conceal something. Dear me! *(Places it at some distance on the floor,)*

F

my brother must have sent it! Somebody that
has a right to do so, the fellow said; that
must be my brother, and so I may look at it.
Besides, my father will certainly send back
the furniture, and then this may bear the rest
company. Now, if I should not even look at
it, it would seem as if I despised my brother.
No, I will open and look at the things; but certainly I will keep none. *(Kneels down, cuts the
strings, opens the lid, and starts up in surprise.)*
Ay dear! how pretty! *(Kneels down again.)*
A cloak! O what beautiful lace! hem! why,
a cloak is not too gay for tradesfolks; I think
it is part of their dress; I may keep it. *(Puts
it on.)* As if it had been made for me!
(Kneels down again.) A hat! a very pretty one
indeed!—but a feather,—no, God forbid!
(Pause.) All but that feather,—I might wear
it without a feather. A new hat, I wonder
how I look in it! *(Puts it on, and then
steps up to the glass.)* Pretty well;—and the
cap under the hat,—that looks like the picture
of the handsome English lady at my brother's.
(Returns to the box.) What is that red stuff?
(Takes out a gown.) Rofe-colour! *(Astonished,
calls out aloud.)* Satin! *(The gown drops on
the floor.)* Satin! God forbid I should wear
satin! That is too gaudy, too glossy, too
shewy; it would draw all the neighbours to
their windows. *(Takes up the gown.)* I hope
I have spoiled nothing. *(Hangs it over a
chair, kneels down, and continues to examine the
box.)*

SCENE VIII.

Enter SOPHIA REISSMAN.

Sophia knocks. Frederica screams, and covers her face with her hands.

Soph. (comes in.) Any good people in this house? *(Fred. rises and curtesies, her eyes cast down.)* They must be all dead, as no one is to be found.

Fred. I am quite alone in the house, madam.

Soph. Do you know me, sweet girl?

Fred. You are, Miss—yes—but—

Soph. Reissman. The Aulic Counsellor Reissman's daughter.

Fred. So; I am glad; I know it well enough; but pray do me the favour to be seated.

Soph. My visit will be but short. I am come to form an acquaintance with the sister of a gentleman who is not indifferent to me, as you may know perhaps.

Fred. We have been told, that he is to have the honour—

Soph. And then I wish to put a question to you, in whose praise I have heard so much, and for whom I entertain great esteem. I expect you will answer it candidly.

Fred. You do me an honour.

Soph. Nothing of that. We are going to be nearer,—nay, very nearly connected with one another. My happiness is concerned in

F 2

that question; and so I had rather hear you say, that the confidence I repose in you gives you pleasure, if it really does so.

Fred. Pardon my surprise. I am not my-self in this moment. I am masqued in a dress that is not suited to my condition in life. My brother has sent it to me. I mean to return the whole. Now I have told you so, I am more easy; and I am now ready to answer every question you may ask with candour.

Soph. Well then, I will candidly own, that I love and esteem your brother for what he is, for what he yet may become, and for what, I hope, he will yet be willing to become. In one respect only I am quite a stranger to him, and in this respect I must remain so, if— and therefore I have applied to you. Upon what footing, pray, are you with him, you and your father?

Fred. We? Upon a good footing! *(After a pause with affected vivacity.)* Oh, upon a very good footing!

Soph. I say no.

Fred. We are, indeed,

Soph. And again I say no. His silence made me suspect him. And you, my good girl, if you were quite satisfied with his con-duct, quite so, as a sister would be with a good brother, you would, in answer to my question, have told me all that love, gratitude, and benevolence, can inspire in one continued strain. You, therefore, are not, at least not particularly so, upon good terms. Whose fault can that be? I am sure not your good father's: report contradicts that; and, I think, I have partly convinced myself of it. Consequently, it is your brother's fault ; and that I do not like.

Fred. Your suppositions crowd so upon me—

Soph. Not my suppositions, but truth. Had you satisfactory truth to return, you would not hesitate so much.

Fred. It may be easily conceived, that the difference of rank between him and us will occasion many trifling differences, for which we blame my brother more than we ought perhaps.

Soph. It may be so partly ;—but then it should be no more than trifling, and as such ought always to be removed by him who has the advantage.

SCENE IX.

Enter GERNAU.

Gernau, startled at Frederica's dress, discovers the satin gown ;—steps forward ; once more looks at Frederica, bows politely to Sophia, and is going to withdraw.

Fred. Stay, if you please.—

Gern. I do not wish to intrude.

Soph. No ceremonies; our conversation is at an end. It is not the last we shall have, I hope. In that case it has been of use, if not to us all, most certainly to me.

Frederica is greatly embarrassed, while Gernau, unable to conceal his chagrin, and to keep his countenance, examines the satin.

Soph. (*observing both.*) If I mistake not, Sir, you have a particular interest that every dress should become this amiable girl;—you certainly are of my opinion, that all the pretty things her brother has just now sent her cannot add to her charms. (*Curtesies to him and to Frederica.*) Good bye. (*Goes.*)

(*Fred. attends her.*)

Soph. (*turns quick round.*) If my visit has proved agreeable, I beg you will not attend me; and you, Sir, may meanwhile confirm, that I am right in my opinion of my young friend. (*Exit quickly.*)

SCENE X.

FREDERICA, GERNAU.

Fred. I shall stay then, dear Friend. What do you think of me? (*Takes off her cloak and hat.*)

Gern. I think I find you quite in the modern stile.

Fred. All sent by my brother.

Gern. Very gallant! and then the furniture, all is strange to me.

Fred. All from my brother.

Gern. What is meant? Perhaps in honour of my departure?

Fred. Departure!—

Gern. I am going to be removed from this place.

Fred. Where to?

Gern. To Freethal.

Fred. Gernau!

Gern. Yes, yes! your brother, I see, has great views concerning this house. O Frederica, I came in such a melancholy mood!—Your gaudy dress, and all this superb furniture, cast such a gloom over my mind.

Fred. You removed? And, when he robs my heart of all that is dear to it, he sends me satin and tinsel, and hopes by that to bribe me? What a mean opinion he must entertain of me! and how I dislike him!

Gern. Frederica, what is to become of me! When we shall be at so great a distance from each other; when, in obedience to my official duties, I muft fly over hill and valley, your picture in my mind, and my heart beating only for you, the image of the poor huntsman will soon be effaced by the splendid objects with which you are going to be dazzled.

Fred. No! and away with the first temptation they have prepared for me; help me to pack up these things; they shall be returned this minute. (*Takes the satin, Gernau helps her to fold it up, and they carry it to the box; she kneels down to put the gown in, whilst he holds the other end; he stoops and looks in the box, and then says,*)

Gern. What is that?

Fred. (*holding up the gown.*) What?

Gern. A pocket-book!

Fred. Put it down. All shall go. I will keep nothing.

Gern. What paper is that, that sticks out there?

Fred. Take it.

Gern. (Pulls out a note.) That is not your brother's hand.

Fred. I have not yet seen that pocket-book.

Gern. Oh, very likely! *(Reads.)* " These dresses are destined to envelope the angel I adore ; accept them as a small token of my sincere affections. *Selling.*"—Take, for my last adieu, contempt, .thou faithless perfidious girl! *(Throws the pocket-book at. her feet, and flies off.)*

Fred. Gernau!

SCENE XI.

Enter Master CLARENBACH.

Clar. What is the matter here?

Fred. Stop him!

Gern. Leave me !—

Clar. (lays hold of him.) Well, stop a moment! What is it? What, *(looks round,)* good heaven, what is all this!

Fred. My brother !—

Gern. (shoving the box towards him.) Coun-sellor Selling!

Clar. Where is my furniture? who had the impudence? who has permitted it? Girl, daughter, Frederica! where was you when all this was done? where is my furniture, my

furniture? What are your intentions, people?
(looking at the box.) What is that, what is it?

Gern. Counsellor Selling's livery.

Fred. An incomprehensible present for me.

Clar. Pack up; lay hold; each of you a
piece; carry it into the passage! Ere night
all shall be packed up, and packed off too.
*(All take a piece of furniture, Gernau takes the
band-box.)* Stop, stop! each two pieces! take
up—*(whilst they are each taking two pieces, he
discovers the easy chair, and shoves it into the
middle of the room.)* So thou art here yet, old
friend! that is right! *(lifts up both his arms.)*
You are the capital of my rank in life; *(giving
a knock against the chair,)* and thou art the
land-mark to point out how far I should extend
the use of that capital. Away with the rest!
away, I say! *(They carry off the furniture.)*

ACT III.

SCENE I.

The Aulic Counsellor REISSMAN'S *House.*

Enter REISSMAN, *with hat and cane.*

Reiss. Not here neither? *(Rings the bell.)*
Where then can she be,—my young lady, my
daughter?

G

Enter SERVANT.

Reiss. Where is my daughter?

Serv. In the garden.

Reiss. Run and tell her to come directly.

Serv. (exit.) Now it is done. *(walking up and down pleased.)* Now it is right, and—*(stops suddenly,)* but that perverse old-fashioned fellow, with his pious lamentations—Pshaw! my intended son-in-law must manage him, and that quickly too, or he shall not have the girl. He is in love with her and the money,—a twofold inducement! He is in my hand, because his conscience is not altogether free,—a triple security!

SCENE II.

Enter SOPHIA.

Soph. You have ordered—

Reiss. I congratulate you, my dear daughter, on your approaching nuptials with the Privy Counsellor. The suit is won; the bequest is confirmed; the money is mine; *Victoria!*

Soph. (coldly.) So?

Reiss. Yes, truly! Well, what does my dear child say?

Soph. You have carried off the prize.

Reiss. Yes! that is what I have just said.

Soph. Then you have attained your wish.

Reiss. Attained your wish! Is that a reply, when 10,000 pounds have fallen to my lot? Is that the behaviour of a daughter to her father on so happy an occasion.

Soph. Dear father, will not you permit me to reflect a little on those that have lost that immense sum.

Reiss. They are entire strangers to us both, no way related to us.

Soph. The legacy was left by a stranger too.

Reiss. And now it is mine; and if thou wilt not rejoice with me—

Soph. Excuse me, I cannot.

Reiss. Then I will call in persons from the street, that they may share my pleasure. *(Pauses.)* Speak, unnatural child, and rejoice!

Soph. I am silent, I do not wish to offend you, I love you with all the tenderness of a dutiful child.

Reiss. Would I had a son that knew how to place a due value on this, to enjoy it, to double it, then it would be worth while! But now, when I wish to enjoy the result of all my plans, and the successes I have met with in all my life, I have your sentimental feelings to encounter; and then I would rather relate my happiness to one of the ever-green pyramids in the garden than to you.

Soph. O heaven!

Reiss. And who is to reap the benefit but you, and you only? When I am gone, you may settle annuities upon all the beggars of the country, travel through the rugged mountains, waste my dear wealth in cottages, and scatter hard dollars like pebbles.

Soph. Give me but a sufficient allowance, restore the remainder to Brunnig's children, and I will thank you on my knees.

Reiss. Indeed! Aye, if I were to give you the money and the bond, to divide among those brats, it would make a nice anecdote in the newspapers. Zounds! I am apt to think, that, when you come to the possession of all my property, you will scarce do so much as to erect a small monument to the memory of your father.

Soph. Alas! Brunnig's children would form the fittest groupe of weeping orphans around such a monument.

Reiss. Ungrateful wretch! is this the return for my parental affection? Was it not through the view of gaining this legacy that I raised a deputy to the rank of a privy counsellor? Who is my wealth to devolve to but you and him?

SCENE III.

Enter Privy Counsellor CLARENBACH.

Reiss. There he is! Thanks, my hearty thanks for the dispatch! That is what I call business. That is what I call a specimen of a useful son-in-law.—Now Miss may fix the happy day. She will tell us more about it at dinner. I will step down to the cellar, and take care that we shall have the best it can afford. We will pour liquid gold down our throats to solemnize the acquisition of solid gold.   [*Exit.*

SCENE IV.

SOPHIA, *Privy Counsellor* CLARENBACH.

Sophia wipes her eyes.

P. Coun. (after a pause.) Why does my dear Sophia weep?

Soph. My father is pleased with you.

P. Coun. I see I am the cause of your grief.

Soph. Does your conscience tell you so?

P. Coun. Your tears do.

Soph. (after a pause.) Well, then, answer my tears.

P. Coun. (shrugs up his shoulders.) The dead letter has decided in this business, as it does in many more, where our feelings would decide in a different manner, but dare not.

Soph. And dare not!—Further—

P. Coun. Further it fills me with the deepest distress to see my Sophia thus distressed. I am not to blame. I would give any thing to alter the circumstance.

Soph. Any thing?—do not be offended at this question. It conveys no doubt. It contains my firmest confidence in the heart of the man to whom I am going to tender mine,—to whom I have tendered it already. Yes, Clarenbach, I do not conceal it from you; I could not leave you without giving myself up to those tears.

P. Coun. Sophia, my angel! the promised companion of my life, my guardian angel, the most precious gift of providence! How dare

I presume to merit your partiality? No! I shall never be able to merit you. Such purity and goodness of mind! how can I convince you of the sincerity of my esteem?

Soph. Clarenbach!

P. Coun. (*takes her by the hand.*) Sophia!

Soph. A wife has many duties to discharge. And I must tell you before hand, I shall never content myself merely to be your wife, unless I am able to influence you and your actions.

P. Coun. To bless those for whom I am to act.

Soph. But what will be my powers over you? I know the first generous impulse of your heart is always good; but then ambition,—let me speak truth to you,—avarice, the offspring of ambition, leads you astray, and contaminates the source of your first feelings.

P. Coun. (*looks aside.*) It is so! (*after a pause.*) Love will buoy me up.

Soph. I shall crave little for myself; but in a just cause I shall at all times insist upon having every thing entire. I shall not relent; the man of my heart must act in full; his actions and motives must appear as clear before the eye of the world as they do in the eye of heaven.—Now the question is, will you, on these conditions, give me your hand? Answer me?

P. Coun. (*drops at his feet.*) Sophia!

Soph. Rise! I expect no answer from love, but from your conviction. Try your own self. The answer, which you are to give me now, is

more than that which you are to give at the
foot of the altar; there we are to exchange
vows, and all will be settled; but here,—by ourselves,—no witnesses but ourselves,—here,
where nothing influences us but the sentiment
of future happiness or sorrow, which we create
to ourselves, and our eternal responsibility,
which, at every motion of the pulse, admo-
nishes us with increased force:—to speak
truth,—here we are to unite our hearts for
ever,—or separate. Once more then I repeat,
on different conditions I will not accept your
hand; am I your choice on these conditions!

P. Coun. Yes, yes, yes! Do not you read in
my eyes that I understand you, that I look up
to you as the source of future bliss; that I repent
the past; that with candour and faith, from
the bottom of my heart, in this delightful solemn moment, I crave your hand, and feel myself quite happy.

Soph. Well my friend, my dear, my beloved
friend! I give credit to all you say, and feel un-
speakably happy; even your failings lie on the
road to rare perfections, and I vow to heaven
that I hope those failings will soon vanish.

P. Coun. You open to me the prospect of
paridisic futurity. I shall be active in the
promoting the benefit of my country, and rise
superior to dirty, narrow, selfish views! recom-
pensed by your approbation, your joys, and
sometimes by your tears. Your gentle hand
shall reach me the petitions of the wretched,
the widow, and the orphan,—and my abilities

shall be called forth in their behalf. O Sophia! our wedding day shall long be remem-
bered by the cottagers; every face shall beam
with smiles.

Soph. May it be so! may we, hand in hand,
conduct our vows pure to the altar, that we
may become securities to each other for our
future happiness. In virtue of your solemn promise, and as your bride, I lay down two conditions previous to our union; if you assent, I will
be your wife, not otherwise.

P. Coun. Speak, that I may have an oppor-
tunity to thank you; to promise and perform.

Soph. The first is, that my father, convinced
by you, shall instantly · resign the legacy
into the hands that ought to receive it.—O
Clarenbach! here the daughter must remain
silent, and your conviction must finish what
would rend my heart! (*Privy Counsellor claps
his hand together.—Sophia continues after a
pause.*) The second condition is, that, as I
feel I demand much, though convinced I could
demand no less,—you shall shorten that state
of uncertainty, and by three o'clock this afternoon bring me an answer on that subject.
You are not to bring it here; but to the place
which this paper (*taking out of her pocket a
sealed paper*) points out. You must not open
it till five minutes before three. Pledge me
your hand.

P. Coun. (*pressing her hand.*) My word of
honour!

Soph. (after a pause, during which she has been gazing on him with tenderness, utters in a steady tone,) Adieu, *(going,)* my friend!

P. Coun. (without parting with her hand.) O Sophia, Sophia! what have you demanded!

Soph. (having gently disengaged her hand.) The Chief Judge of my country cannot wish to give me the hand which signed the deed that robs orphans of their right! And, if he thinks he has performed his duty as a judge, let him blush as a man, if he means to conduct me and the spoil at one and the same time to his house. If the man, whom I and the people honour, cannot feel so, the sentiment of my own worth will teach me how to forget him. [*Exit.*

P. Coun. Sophia,—girl,—soul, to which I know no equal! thou hast raised and again precipitated me to the deepest abyss. You shewed me a glimpse of heaven, and then veiled the bright view from my enraptured sight. Noble, kind, cruel girl! Oh, I could weep as I did in the first impression of love! *(throws himself in a chair.)* I could weep virtuous tears! Oh! what now am I, what do I now feel! O the power of pure love!—without thee I cannot exist. *(Starts up.)* Sophia! better being! forget the past, build thy requests upon the future; they commit murder on thy father and me! *(Going, meets Counsellor Wellenberg at the door.)*

H

SCENE V.

Privy Counsellor CLARENBACH, *Counsellor*
WELLENBERG.

Well. Most honoured Sir.

P. Coun. What is your pleasure, Sir?

Well. I am forced, by necessity, to go in quest of you, Sir; the suit of the poor orphans—

P. Coun. Is determined; the will is confirmed.

Well. I know. (*Pulls out a paper.*) This is the decree. The oftener I peruse it, and the longer I consider it, the more it resembles a poor chest forced open, beat to pieces, and in the end carried off.

P. Coun. You grow impertinent, Sir.

Well. No, most honoured Sir! but I am filled with spirit and courage, like an old trusty servant, armed with perseverance and justice in the cause of the orphan, which calls aloud to heaven for redress. That I am, and that you will find me.

P. Coun. Do you intend to appeal?

Well. Yes, I do, indeed.

P. Coun. Well, do so, and leave me.

Well. No, no; I will not leave you. I appeal to you, most honoured Sir, not *qua judex*, but *qua homo, qua homo*, who believes in the day of judgment, and, at the sound of the last trump, would wish to be called to the right; not to be left among the damned, where many an Aulic Counsellor will be found, I am afraid.

P. Coun. I honour the feelings that animate you, Sir; but they are foreign to the affair. Appeal in form, at—

Well. To avoid all *replicas, duplicas, et fatalia,* that may delay and put off the cause, I will put you an *argumentum,* that, *eo ipso,* shall invalidate your sentence, and re-instate the poor children in their right, assigned to them by God and justice.

P. Coun. (*pauses.*) Are you possessed of such an argument? (*With surprise.*) It will be welcome.

Well. Indeed! what you should call truly welcome?—

P. Coun. By heaven, very welcome!

Well. Then give me the embrace of a good man, (*Privy Counsellor goes to embrace him,*) without touching my hands, which at this present time labour under the *chiragra.* (*Embraces him.*) So our town has doubted your humanity, and been of opinion that it is detained as a prisoner in a gold purse.—You blush;—well, that for a Privy Counsellor is a good sign; I will circulate it among the multitude. Now my *argumentum* is, that—

SCENE VI.

Enter Aulic Counsellor REISSMAN.

Reiss. Ay, see there our old honest friend Wellenberg. (*Shakes him by the hand.*)

Well. Oh!—oh dear, oh dear! that God—

Reiss. What is the matter?

Well. (puts one hand in his bosom.) Quoad, old and honest? Yes, *Quoad,* friend?—The *status amicitiæ* case cannot exist; for, if that were the case, you ought to have known that I am afflicted with the *chiragra,* and not to have squeezed my hands so as to make me cry out in such harsh tones, for which I ought to crave, and do crave, pardon of my most honoured Sir.

P. Coun. A particular circumstance has taken place. The gentleman thinks he has found an argument that will invalidate the sentence pronounced in the cause of the disputed legatees, and re-instate the heirs of Brunnig in that property.

Reiss. What?

Well. Yes, it is so. Doctor Kannenfeld, namely, has been visited by heaven with a severe fit of illness, and brought near the gates of death. Moved by the exhortations of his spiritual director, he sent for me to attend, and, amidst tears and groans, confessed that he has deprived the children of their lawful property—

P. Coun. What is that?

Reiss. (frightened.) How?

Well. Being, by a certain *quidam,* whom the finger of heaven, whilst we are here speaking about the matter, has severely touched, persuaded, and bribed, partly to conceal, and even partly to deny the insanity of the testatrix, at the time when the will was made, which robs the true heirs of their due.

P. Coun. (*in a low voice.*) My God! (*Passes.*) *Well.* It is so.

Reiss. (*embarrassed.*) Is Doctor Kannenfeld ill? Ay, ay?

Well. He is very ill. He has stated and deposed all the particulars concerning the certain *quidam.*

Reiss. Well,—and,—

Well. Ay, if I were in your stead, I would say to myself, " True, I have won the cause, but I will not keep what is not mine;" your conscience then would applaud you, and your fellow-citizens would esteem you; you would find consolation under every affliction, and when the cold hand of death had arrested almost every faculty, and benumbed almost every sense, your soul would look up with trembling confidence to heaven. The poor orphans would gather round your dying bed, and weep for their second father. Thus speaks old Wellenberg, gentlemen, whose life has been spent in settling the disputes of this world according to the mild precepts of christianity, a religion that at once consults our happiness here and hereafter.

[*Exit.*

P. Coun. (*to Reissman.*) For heaven's sake!

Reiss. Poh! no matter. (*Calls after Wellenberg.*) Mr. Wellenberg!

Well. (*turns round, without however coming back.*) Well ? *Pœnitet me?*

Reiss. What ails Dr. Kannenfeld?

Well. A burning fever.

Reiss. So? Ho ho! A burning fever!—ha, ha, ha! old gentleman!—and his intellects? When a man lies in a raging fever, and denounces honest people, what credit ought to be attached to it?

Well. In lucidis intervallis ?

Reiss. Burning fever is only another word for madness; the denunciations of a madman is valid only with madmen.

Well. Shall I take them in the presence of witnesses? Shall the faculty make an affidavit of the state of his mind?

Reiss. Do as you please.

Well. And should he die and leave such a deposition?

Reiss. Then it is the deposition of a madman.

Well. Hem! (*musing.*) And if, aided by all the courts, I were to put you to an oath concerning the foul means you employed to get that will made in your favour—

Reiss. What then?

Well. Then you will—

P. Coun. It is a disagreeable affair I see; and Mr. Reissman has already declared that at all events he was disposed, through mere benevolence, to give up part of the legacy.

Reiss. What?

Well. What he means to do, let him do in full, and not by halves.

Reiss. Nothing; not a single penny! as you want to compel me, not a single penny! Your sick madman is a calumniator, and so—

Well. *Vera laus est laudari a viro laudato.*

Reiss. Now, do not rouze my passion, but get you gone. In writing, do as you think proper; I shall know what to do on my side.

Well. *Fiat!*—Then I will set to work, that the judgment of God may be made manifest on the unjust. [*Exit.*

SCENE VII.

Privy Counsellor CLARENBACH, *Aulic Counsellor* REISSMAN.

P. Coun. (*confused.*) Sir, you see me so perplexed—

Reiss. Do not you talk, you have spoiled all.

P. Coun. I will run after him.

Reiss. You shall not, Sir.

P. Coun. You are undone.

Reiss. Who says so?

P. Coun. God forbid you should take the oath.

Reiss. Instead of standing there by the side of that insect of the law, like a scholar that has received a wrap over his knucles, you ought to have thundered him down with the voice of a judge, with influence and authority.

P. Coun. But I knew nothing of those shocking circumstances before.

Reiss. Hem! As if there was any difference between persuading a foolish woman to make a will, or getting a fellow that is half mad to draw it up. The former, however, you have supposed to be the case, and yet your morality sustained no shock.

P Coun. But the oath?—

Reiss. Your pretended delicacy of conscience revolts at it; the mere cowardice of a boy. Who are you, that now takes the part of conscience against me? Are you a better man than I?

P. Coun. Whose work is it?

Reiss. You are a greater coward, but not the better man. Do not presume to raise yourself an inch above me. You have sold both right and bread.

P. Coun. Sir, the pupil may yet recede.

Reiss. If the master will let him; ·but the master holds him in his hand. If he recedes, mind that he must shrink into his original insignificance. He must hide from this world, for I—I shall not fall alone. If I fall, the ground around shall tremble! Do you take me?

P. Coun. Horrid and abominable!

Reiss. Perhaps you imagine, that I have transformed the carpenter's son into a privy counsellor, merely for the sake of having him for a son-in-law? or because you are master of a tolerable good stile? No, you shall serve me, because you are both good enough and bad enough for the purpose.

P. Coun. But I will not, I will not! I say, with all the resolution, with all the exertion of every one of those good feelings which you would sear and benumb.

Reiss. Too late. You are so entangled, that you can neither advance nor recede. You are fixed where I have placed you.—Thus much for the present. Now leave me in my native good humour. As to the old lawyer, I can soon manage him, never fear.—Get the better of your squeamish conscience, and come to dinner.

P. Coun. I cannot.

Reiss. I desire it,—I insist upon it.

SCENE VIII.

Enter COUNSELLOR SELLING.

Sell. Miss has sent me up;—dinner is on the table.

Reiss. Come, gentlemen.

Sell. You have won the day.

Reiss. Undoubtedly. .

Sell. I wish you joy.

Reiss. Now here is the Privy Counsellor, who puzzles his head about some talk concerning the will.

Sell. Ah, that should not puzzle me.

Reiss. Beati possidentes! Either, or—

P. Coun. Or!—there is the rub.

SCENE IV.

Enter MASTER CLARENBACH.

Clar. With your permission, gentlemen, I want to speak with my son.

Reiss. By yourselves?

Clar. Hem!—I should think so!

Reiss. Well, then do not let us wait long. *(to the Privy Counsellor, half audible.)* You have

I

understood, me sufficiently, I think. — Servant, Master Clarenbach. Come along, Counsellor.   [*Exeunt.*

SCENE X.

PRIVY COUNSELLOR, MASTER CLAREN-
BACH.

Clar. I must come to you once more;—have
you seen old Wellenberg?

P. Coun. Yes.

Clar. Well, what do you say about it?

P. Coun. I am shocked.

Clar. Thank God! What do you mean to
do?

P. Coun. Alas! what can I do?

Clar. Jack, your honour is already in great
arrears with our town, and your conscience
does not altogether keep a fair day-book. I
ask you, in the name of God, what do you
mean to do?

P. Coun. All I can, father!

Clar. If you are in earnest, come along with
me; let us go from hence.

P. Coun. Why so soon,—and whither?

Clar. Fly, fly from the brink of destruction.
You must not dine here, you must not remain
here any longer. You must not marry into
this family.

P. Coun. The girl is my good genius. I
cannot leave her.

Clar. Then her father, that bad genius, will
not leave you! Do not struggle between the

two. Come along with me; do as you ought;
be afraid of no man, confide in God, and hope!
You will have the girl at last. Come along
with me.

P. Coun. I wish I could! were I not at once
rivetted down here by the demon of evil,
and irresistibly bid to stay by the power of
virtue!

Clar. Jack, dear Jack, my son, do not send
me away without you; come along with me.

P. Coun. I cannot; you see I cannot.

Clar. God have mercy on thee! thou art undone!

P. Coun. It may be. I am undone whether
I stay or go. And so I will stay and strive,
and see what I can yet retrieve of my honour.

Clar. How can you save the honour of your
situation in life, if the honour of your heart be
lost, and that must be lost among these people?
—You have removed honest Gernau, because
he acts up to his duty.—Your sister weeps bit-
terly,—the town despises you;—I have not yet
frowned on you, and will not do so now, because I pity you. But I will leave this town,
and take shelter with honest Gernau, who is
to be my son-in-law.

P. Coun. You will leave this town?

Clar. I do not wish it. I shall, with tears,
leave my timber-yard and the work which
hitherto I have carried on with pleasure and
success. But as there is no remedy to save
you from destruction, I must go. I cannot
witness it.

60 THE LAWYERS,

P. Coun. Is it my fault, if—

Clar. Your faults are many and great; your native town knows them, and despises you. I cannot see you lowered thus, Jack. It has not been in my power to make a great man of you, but I have educated you to be an honest man. I have taken care of the tree, while young, and now it is grown up, one branch decays after the other. And if it must be so, that no green sprig shall henceforth flourish, then I will turn my eyes from it, visit it no more, nor live on the spot where the withered stem, that I am so fond of, shall fall.

P. Coun. Father!

Clar. I cannot weep; but I feel myself very ill on your account.

Enter a Servant.

Serv. The company is waiting for the Privy Counsellor.

P. Coun. I am coming.   [*Exit Servant.*

Clar. Dear son, do not let me go without you. Behold! you may still go with me as half a good man; we will all strive to mend the other bad half.—Have pity on yourself and me; you stand, upon my word, on the spot where the road divides,—the bad people in there, and here your old father. They hold out to you good and high life; I offer you peace and happiness.—For God's sake, Jack, follow me!

P. Coun. (*embraces him.*) I cannot do that; but I vow to you I will yet do much.

Clar. That is a good word, and no more. Farewell, I will set off.—I shall not see you again. Once more give me your hand,

P. Coun. No, I shall not do that. I will not part with you in this manner.

Clar. It is best so;—it shakes my whole frame,—and my daughter has likewise a claim on my life! Come then once more to this heart, that once delighted in you.—(*Embraces him.*)

P. Coun, Father!—

Clar. You weep over yourself! God! that it should come to this!—Now farewell; I forgive thee, and so does thy sister. May God take thy wealth from thee, that thou mayest amend, and sometime leave this world in peace!—Farewell! (*Attempts to go.*)

SCENE XI.

Enter Aulic Counsellor REISSMAN.

Reiss. Well, we are waiting.

Clar. (*pulling his son towards him.*) You would take him away from me,—tear him out of my arms,—drag him away!—he is my son, and no father will tamely suffer his son to precipitate himself into perdition. Jack, I will not leave thee, I will not yield thee up!—Thou art mine, nature and thy heart have closely interwoven us together; wilt thou, of thy own accord, leave me?

P, Coun. (*throws his arms round him.*) No, I cannot;—I will follow you hence!

Clar. God be praised, my son is saved!

[*Exeunt arm in arm.—Reissman follows them a few steps, sets his arms a-kembow, and looks after them.*

ACT IV.

SCENE I.

Aulic Counsellor Reissman's, the same rooom as in the preceding act.

Aulic Counsellor REISSMAN *enters in a passion;* SOPHIA *follows.*

Reiss. Not a word, not a word more, not a single syllable of that silly fool! What, to leave me and you, as if we were infected with the plague and breathed contagion? I cannot bear the affront, it shall not go unavenged. I had rather die a thousand deaths.

Soph. Was it not his father that desired him to go with him? and you know he ought to obey him.

Reiss. Who am I, and what is his father? Do not name him any more in my hearing; you must not see him any more, nor even think of him. That petty Privy Counsellor is now dead and buried to me.

Soph. By your advice I listened to his addresses.

Reiss. Forget him then by my command.

SCENE II.

Enter Servant.

Serv. Grobman, the ironmonger.

Reiss. Very well, very well; shew him in.

[*Exit Servant.*

Reiss. (to Sophia.) You may retire, go!

Soph. Your commands.   [*Exit.*

Reiss. Fie upon him! a creature that I raised from obscurity!—a fellow, who eight years ago was a petty fogger, whom I have raised to the rank of a Privy Counseller!—I was a fool when I did so;—such a fellow soar over my head! (*Stamps with his foot.*) I would sooner see the whole frame of nature dissolve. I will not lose sight of my object; I will proceed with spirit and caution. I have raised the useless pile, I will pull it down again.

SCENE III.

Enter GROBMAN.

Reiss. (calm and friendly.) What is your pleasure, dear Mr.——?

Grob. Benniger has obtained the monopoly.

Reiss. You do not say so, do you?

Grob. The Privy Counsellor is to procure it for 2300 dollars, which sum is to be paid this afternoon.

Reiss. Impossible!

Grob. It is but too true. The money is to be paid to Counsellor Selling.

Reiss. (confidentially.) I must tell you that Selling has already mentioned something to me about it. The young man's conscience is alarmed. He does not like to lend a hand in those sort of things. But I would not believe it.

Grob. It is but too certain.

Reiss. O Lord! who could think any thing

like it of such a man? that is mean, that is—
that must not be permitted. Ay, ay! and
the minister prefers such a man, reposes confidence in him, because men, like me, take him
by the hand. They think, because such a man
is of a low extraction, he must have the interest of the lower class at heart. And then he
will betray and sell the state!

Grob. As an inhabitant, I ought to have the
preference to a stranger.

Reiss. Most undoubtedly.

Grob. I am very willing to go to some ex-
pence too, only—

Reiss. Not a single penny; God forbid I
should be guilty of such a sin! That contract
with Benniger must be annulled.

Grob. If that were possible, I would with all
my heart—

Reiss. Ay, it must be so. I am very inti-
mate with the Privy Counsellor. He was to
have my daughter; but I will never give her to
a man like him. You must furnish me immediately with a plea, in which you must deve-
lope the whole transaction.

Grob. Good God! the Privy Counsellor!

Reiss. I give you my word and hand, as an
honest man, I will run all the consequences.
In such a case one is in conscience bound; only
let me have the declaration immediately. I
will manage in such a manner that the Privy
Counsellor shall come off with tolerable good
credit.

Grob. If you will do that—

Reiss. Yes, yes, yes!

Grob. But Counsellor Selling—

Reiss. Is a young man;—out of fear of displeasing the Privy Counsellor, he has lent his aid. Such a young man may yet be taught in time. That is my principal object.

Grob. Well, the declaration shall be drawn up without delay. Heaven bless you, dear Sir, for thus taking the part of a poor fellow-townsman! [*Exit.*

Reiss. My duty, my duty!—Bravo, little Selling, that is prettily managed!

SCENE IV.

Enter Counsellor SELLING.

Sell. Old Wellenberg wishes to call on you.

Reiss. Has he taken any steps yet with the Doctor, concerning the mad patient?

Sell. No, the Doctor is breathing his last.

Reiss. If God should call him off, the calumniator will escape a very serious action in this world. Now my claims and the will have been confirmed, I will, of my own accord, make the children a handsome present.

Sell. Very laudable!

Reiss. When is Benniger to bring you the present for the Privy Counsellor?

Sell. Very soon, I expect.

Reiss. Take it, that we may have a proof; then tell Benniger your mind, and open the business to me.

Sell. But then I fear the Privy Counsellor will take it in dudgeon.

K

Reiss. The Privy Counsellor! I will silence him with a single look; ask me within a fortnight what the Privy Counsellor says,—ask me then what he is. God! could I ever have dreamt of any such thing, when I was raising and supporting that upstart!

Sell. Every one is astonished at your condescension and kindness.

Reiss. All disinterestedness! all good-nature! Was I not going to give him my child? but God forbid!—he does not deserve her.

Sell. Every one knows that you are in the highest favour with the Ministry—

Reiss. These many years.—

Sell. That, properly speaking, you govern both the Privy Counsellor and the whole country.

Reiss. I know the country and the people.

Sell. To please you, I attached myself to the Privy Counsellor; but his vanity is such that I cannot hold out with him any longer. He has this very day told me that I learned nothing.

Reiss. There we have it.—

Sell. That I did not know my own language; that I made a motion in court so ridiculous the other day, that every one laughed at me; nay, he told me to my face that I attempted to assume an air of importance that I was not entitled to.

Reiss. I am shocked at it, do you know? Your dear father, who is now no more, was a man who—

Sell. Was Privy Counsellor! But that is
nothing in his eyes. Such an upstart will
press forward, and people of our consequence
must render homage not only to him, but even
to the carpenter's family.

Reiss. Pray, were not you to marry his
sister?

Sell. No, no! yet, in the state of subjection
he kept me, he might at last have brought me
to it. He would, as he calls it, correct my
writings, and then he would, by way of making
it up, sometimes nod his head by way of approbation.

Reiss. As I see that the fellow does not deserve what I have done for him, all shall be
altered in future: attach yourself to me.

Sell. Good God! I will with both my hands.

Reiss. I will make out the draft for the declaration, in which you are to charge him with
having taken a bribe, and also for having constantly forced you to vote as he pleased in the
court. I will carry my point; the Prime Minister shall be informed of the whole. Go
hence, and I will send you every thing.

Sell. I shall be very glad to get rid of him;
but you will assist me occasionally to propose
a law too? will you not?

Reiss. By way of practising? oh yes!

Sell. No, a real law, according to which the
people are to act, be it ever so trifling,—only
that the world may know, that I can frame a
law as well as another. I only want it for the
sake of the world, and the consequence it will
give me. [*Exit.*

Reiss. A shallow, shallow, ignorant boy!—
but then he may be of use to me.

SCENE V.

Enter Privy Counsellor CLARENBACH.

P. Coun. I have to explain to you, Sir.

Reiss. Just as you like, Sir.

P. Coun. I cannot remain the man, that,
God knows how,—I have gradually—

Reiss. I think so myself.

P. Coun. I can be dependent on you no longer;
but I do not choose to be ungrateful. Without
enquiring into the motives which induced you
to raise me, I owe you my grateful thanks for
having done so.

Reiss. I am hourly more and more convinced that I ought to have done so.

P. Coun. This sarcastic remark shall not
prevent me, as your intended son-in-law, to
render you my services from the purest motives
and filial zeal, and to endeavour to compromise
that disagreeable affair respecting the will.

Reiss. Ay! would you indeed?

P. Coun. If we only consider it as politically
pernicious, it—

Reiss. There is nothing pernicious in the
whole affair, my affectionate Mr. Privy Counsellor, and your services are quite useless.

P. Coun. I wish they may prove so. Meanwhile you will not misinterpret my intentions.

Reiss. Your intentions go to the future inheritance of my property, my son-in-law that
would be.—

P. Coun. Your daughter,—without any inheritance whatever—

Reiss. With or without inheritance, that is all over; you shall not have her.

P. Coun. You may disinherit her, if you please, should I receive her hand against your will; but your daughter is mine according to your promise, and you can shew no cause for breaking it.

Reiss. (*coldly.*) Oh yes!

P. Coun. What? which?

Reiss. Some other time.

P. Coun. When? I desire to know it. I desire it, I tell you.

Reiss. You shall soon know it if you are in such a hurry.—I am now busy.

P. Coun. Sir, if Sophia were not your daughter—

Reiss. Ah, that is the thing. Go, your papa is waiting for you:—if you stay, he will come and take you away.

P. Coun. Sir!

Reiss. And come to save you too. Has not he saved you once already this very day?—

P. Coun. Yes, he has that, honest man! May heaven reward him for it!

Reiss. He may perhaps save you once more yet, and perhaps not.—Meanwhile, give yourself no farther trouble to call here. Your servant, Sir.

P. Coun. (*looks at his watch.*) You distress me more than you know. If that can give you pleasure, enjoy it. [*Exit.*

Reiss. (*looking after him.*) Hem! I ought to have discovered at first sight that the fellow is not fit for my purpose; he is simple enough to be in love in right earnest.—My foolish daughter loves him too; she fans his hopes, so of course he will not injure me, when cashiered. The Doctor is falling asleep, and the Lawyer, —hem!—must likewise be sent to rest,—else I shall have no rest myself!   [*Exit.*

SCENE VI.
Master Clarenbach's house.

Master CLARENBACH, FREDERICA, *and* GER-NAU, *busy with bringing in the furniture seen in the first Act.*

Clar. Courage, my dear children! about it! Thank God, we have got rid of that fashionable trumpery. Set the table again there in its place.—So!—how glad I am to behold my old friends again!

Fred. We shall have a comfortable repast on that table to night.

Clar. As Jack is to be one of the party, O yes!

Gern. I hope his change is right earnest; but I can scarcely believe it.

Clar. No reflections, dear Gernau! What is past ought to be forgotten.

Gern. But I must remove hence for all that.

Clar. Why, perhaps not. Jack will now employ his power to some good purpose.

Fred. I wonder where he stays so long.

Clar. He is dissolving the partnership of sin with Reissman.

Gern. I wish it may be done in writing.

Clar. I have insisted on his having a conversation with him.

SCENE VII.

Enter SOPHIA.

Clar. Whom have I the honour to—(*Bows, and all the rest rise.*)

Soph. Without ceremony, my friends.

Fred. It is Miss Reissman, father!

Soph. Give me leave to wait for your son, Sir, who is to introduce me to your acquaintance. (*To Frederica.*) We have seen one another already.

Clar. Miss Reissman? So—(*with a smile.*) The daughter of Mr. —; do not take it amiss.

Soph. What?

Fred. Father, let it rest there.

Clar. Yes, yes! We do not like to mention any thing about it. You, you are welcome wherever you go; and so you are to me, God knows! Sit down here near an old man, if you have no objection. (*Gern. reaches her a chair.*)

Soph. I know how to value the honour of this seat.

Clar. You have a good opinion of my son.

Soph. Yes, good Sir.

Clar. He is rather in an odd predicament to day; but I hope things will take a better turn.

Soph. I sincerely hope so, good father.

SCENE VIII.

Enter Privy Counsellor CLARENBACH.

P. Coun. I am happy to find you, Sophia, by the side of my good father, hand in hand. What an enchanting picture in my eye! love, worth, and affection, hand in hand! my Sophia beneath the same roof under which I was born!

Soph. Yes; and I read in your eyes that you were pleased to see me here.

P. Coun. (kissing her hand.) God is my witness, this moment is the happiest of my life; happiness has been a stranger to my heart this long time.

Soph. (rises.) Let peace and happiness dwell in this house henceforward; the good intelligence which I intended to bring about between father and son, between brother and sister, and friend, has taken place without any interference;—so much the better!

Clar. Ay, I see that your good intentions were in my favour. They were good I see,—I thank you for them. Give me your hand, sweet creature! *(shaking her good naturedly by the hand.)* Blessed is the man who is doomed to have you for his wife.

Soph. Happy is that son who has such a father! *(She leads the son up to the father, and they embrace.)*

P. Coun. Behold the father of us both, Sophia!

Soph. O heaven!

P. Coun. How!

Soph. That is the grand question that must give us pause! *(Clarenbach makes a sign to Frederica and Gernau, and they retire with him.)*

SCENE IX.

SOPHIA, *Privy Counsellor* CLARENBACH.

P. Coun. I have fulfilled one of your conditions. The other—

Soph. You have lost all your influence over my father.

P. Coun. Yes!

Soph. Then my condition is too hard,—I cancel it.

P. Coun. Heaven bless you !

Soph. I will substitue an other in its place, which depends entirely on yourself.

P. Coun. Then it is already accomplished.

Soph. Am I your choice even without any inheritance?

P. Coun. Without any inheritance whatever!

Soph. Your hand and heart are all I crave. To be candid, I expected nothing less from you. Now for the arduous question; hear me ! The disposition in which I find you to day is charming, but not meritorious. You have not been moulded to it by virtue, but frightened into it by vice. You are irritable, you are weak, you are ambitious. A time may come, when nei-

L.

ther your father, nor the woman you love will
be able to influence you, as they luckily do at
present.

P. Coun. You wrong me.

Soph. No, my friend. Give me time to proceed. You are irritable, weak, and ambitious!
Do you think, that, on the summit which you
now stand, you can render yourself useful to
your fellow subjects with these three—I had
almost called them vices.

P. Coun. Not if I remain as I am.

Soph. You have hitherto been the instrument
of strangers, and, in proportion as you rose in
extrinsic pomp, you sunk in intrinsic merit.

P. Coun. True, it is too true.

Soph. You are not possessed of sufficient resolution to stand at the helm of a government;
but you have genius, a good heart, and learning enough, sufficient to secure a tranquil passage through life. Let my love supply the
whole of my father's considerable fortune; I
cannot muster the requisite resolution. Can
your esteem for me induce you to renounce the
gilded splendor of state and office, and to
spend the remainder of your days in the calm
retirement of obscurity? *(Eagerly.)* Have you
the resolution, Clarenbach, to resign the Privy
Counsellorship?—I do not want an immediate
answer.

P. Coun. Love shakes my resolution! but to
resign, would it not lower me in the public
eye?

Soph. Would it lower you in your own mind?

P. Coun. No. But—

Soph. Contentment must dwell here. *(Pointing to his heart.)* If ever you have felt content, I need say no more.

P. Coun. No! Oh no!

Soph. Who can refuse his esteem to the man who has tasted the cup of luxury, and, in the flower of youth and in the height of his career, can dash it from his lips, and say, " I will not drink it; I prefer the charms of a tranquil life to all the noise and well-bred hate of a court? I am too irritable to rule my fellow-citizens, notwithstanding I wish to serve them."

P. Coun. Sophia !

Soph. Numbers are anxious to aspire to places, for which they are neither qualified by nature nor education, and, when they have once tasted the sweets of office, how difficult to resign!—I know it.

P. Coun. You shake my resolution.

Soph. But if I have not convinced you, then I will not proceed.

P. Coun. Yes, you convince me; but—

Soph. But you do not see what road to pursue after you shall have resigned your bewitching offer? O my friend! whatever may be the choice of your future pursuits, whatever may be the burthen, my heart, my hands, will bear a part in it; I will joyfully, nay with rapture, assist you in **rearing** the fabric of your happiness, of your **tranquil** and real grandeur. Here or elsewhere, merchant, tutor, lawyer, or farmer, whatever you pitch upon, that may afford maintenance and peace of mind, choose that for you and me. I do not wish to have any other share in your determination but the silent satisfaction of having, by inward peace of mind, preserved the life of a good man, whom exterior shew was rapidly conducting to a state of splendid misery.

P. Coun. You have gained your point!—I shall resign my gown. Peace, toil, in future, provided I can call thee my guardian angel!

Soph. (*embraces him.*) I hope you will find me such.

P. Coun. Father, father!—Sophia, thou hast restored me to myself!—but what is to be thy reward?

SCENE X.

Enter MASTER CLARENBACH.

Clar. What is the matter, my son?

P. Coun. Can you conceive it, father? I shall not be a Privy Counsellor much longer.

Clar. How so?

P. Coun. I will lay down my gown, and, with heart and soul, work as I did, before I was raised to that office.

Clar. In earnest? can I rely on it?

P. Coun. Sophia has resigned her fortune on my account, and I shall resign it on hers; —I do not wish for any high office! I am going to re-enter the tranquil class of the industrious citizens. She consents to be my wife. It is her wish, and I see peace and happiness spring from out of it.

Soph. Does it meet with your approbation, father?

Clar. Ay! You ought to read it in my countenance; I would fain open the window, and call out, Jack is no more a Privy Counsellor,— *vivat!* And then there is a pretty, amiable, discreet young lady, that is not possessed with the demon of pride,—*vivat!* and she will be Master Clarenbach's daughter in law,—*vivat!* huzza, I say, Gernau! Girl, come, give me a kiss! *(They kiss.)*

SCENE XI.

Enter GERNAU *and* FREDERICA.

Clar. Jack is my son once more,—*vivat!* huzza! husband and wife! *(steps between them,)* son and daughter! *(Embraces him.)*

Fred. What?

Gern. How?

Clar. More of it another time.

P. Coun. I will resign.

Clar. Look you here, my sweet girl! he was not calculated for it, no more than a true genuine christian Privy Counsellor is calculated for a carpenter. He has had some learning indeed; but then all that solid by-work, such as is requisite for a Privy Counsellor, of that he never was possessed; and so sit down to work. I must work too; we will scrape plenty of money together, without wronging any one. Daughter-in-law, Frederica, and I, will nurse

him as the best soul we know. Now pray give
the girl a kiss, that I may believe in the rela-
tionship.—*(Sophia kisses her.)*—And Jack too,
that I may be quite happy!—*(Sophia gives him a
kiss.)*—And so God bless you in your pursuits!

Soph. (to the Privy Counsellor.) My father
will be your father; and, if ever he could forget
it, spare him, and treat him with filial affection.

P. Coun. I promise it. I shall apply once
more for his consent, which I once obtained.

Fred. Before you resign?

Clar. No, that were a cheat.—But, dear
Jack, all,—how shall I call it? *(half audible,)*
all the earnings of unjust Privy Counsellors,—
return them to whom they may belong, then
you can work with heart-felt satisfaction.

SCENE XII.

Enter Aulic Counsellor REISSMAN.

Reiss. So, I must look for my young lady
here?

Clar. Where she has been doing a deal of
good. Come, Sir, come this way; partake in
the joys of good men, and think you are one of
them.

Soph. Be moved by what you see; sanctify
it by your blessing, and you will make us all
happy.

P. Coun. Yes, Sir.

Clar. Recollect yourself, and act in a good
and fair manner; for, upon my soul! you can-

not go from hence but altogether good or bad;
I tell you that before hand.

Reiss. *(to the Privy Counsellor.)* You have
sold a monopoly to Benniger, Mr. Privy Counsellor.

Clar. There now. Curse that money!

Reiss. One of our citizens has lodged a complaint about it against you.

Clar. Jack, return the wages of sin!

P. Coun. Immediately, and—

Reiss. Of course, and—

Clar. And then it is all over; for I must tell
you, he will not fill the office of a Privy Counsellor any longer.

P. Coun. Yes, Sir, I intend to give in my resignation this very day.

Reiss. Well, well; but your responsibility
for the performance of your duty hitherto, and
the unconscientious—

Soph. Dear father!

P. Coun. Mr. Reissman!

Clar. I hope, you will not make that an object of minute enquiry?

Reiss. That depends on the nature of the
remaining charges. A resignation cannot undo
what is done. Come along, daughter, let
us go.

Soph. Dear father!

P. Coun. In virtue of your promise, you are
my father-in-law; if you wish to be my enemy
in earnest, you may abide by the consequence.
Whatever I could do and urge against you,

Sophia has my word for it, I will do nothing.
Sophia is my lawful bride.

Reiss. By no means, never!

Soph. I am his bride, father; you gave your
word.

Reiss. Before he was impeached.

Fred. Sir—

Gern. (passionately.) That is too much!

Clar. Hush, Sir! or I will run and fetch all
the children of Brunnig, that have been robbed
by you; their words, their tears, and their
curses, shall impeach you before God and man.
You accuse others, who are angels of light
compared with you.

Reiss. (in a passion.) Do you intend to marry
him?

Soph. Yes!

Reiss. Without office, without bread, without honour?

Soph. Without office, without bread, but
who says without honour?

Reiss. I, I, I!

Clar. Thunder and lightning!

P. Coun. Patience, father!—Withdraw; your
daughter stays with my father.

Reiss. If she chooses to be disinherited.

Soph. Be it, in the name of God!

Reiss. I will shew her who is the man for
whom she sacrifices her inheritance.

P. Coun. Then I will inform the world who
has made such a man of me; whose contrivance
it is, if ever I acted contrary to those principles
of honesty this worthy citizen had taught me.

Reiss. What!

Soph. Clarenbach, he is my father!—Clarenbach, where do I stand now?

P. Coun. Would you forsake me, helpless, on the brink of the precipice from which you were just about to snatch me? Do you value my soul less than my honour?

Soph. No, no! I will stay and support you. You have my word; I will not break it.

Reiss. His disgrace shall break it, and distress punish it; you shall never see my face again.

[*Exit.*

Soph. Father!—

Clar. Here is one that has a heart for the distressed children! Come, my daughter.

P. Coun. My resignation was to be spontaneous; it is now forced and attended with disgrace.

Soph. My heart is Clarenbach's, whether he be fortunate or unfortunate.

P. Coun. He will ruin me, and endeavour to dissolve our mutual tie.

Clar. But I and old Wellenberg say, he shall not; between us two old boys we will sing him such a song, as will make him wish he were under earth or water. Let me alone; your happiness is at stake.

Soph. He is my father,—he is old; for his daughter's sake do not disgrace him.

Clar. But disgrace myself, ay? No; honour to him who honour deserves! I will ring the bell of disgrace over him, so as to make the

M

whole country resound. *(Disengages himself, and exit.]*

Soph. On that condition I cannot be your wife. *(Going.)*

P. Coun. *(stops her.)* Sophia!

Soph. In this case, the voice of nature should over-rule that of love! If he is to be ruined, were it to break my heart and cost me my life, it is my duty to perish by his side. *(Disengages herself, and exit.)*

Fred. Sister, dear sister! *(Follows.)*

P. Coun. *(to Gernau.)* Man! you, that, though poor and low, have remained faithful to your duty, I apply to that heart which my power has tortured, and seek for consolation. *(Clings round his neck.)*

Gern. I sympathize in your sufferings; let me go and get information, and act for you.

P. Coun. No! If I should fall, I ought to rise by myself, and if I cannot bring that about, I ought to perish in the dark, unpitied by man.

[*Exit.*

ACT V.

SCENE I.

Enter Aulic Counsellor REISSMAN, *bringing in two bottles of wine, which he puts on the table.*

Reiss. The doctor is dead,—good night to him! The lawyer will soon follow; he is an old man! Old people are subject to many accidents; death has them constantly at his nod, such is the course of nature!

SCENE II.

Enter Counsellor SELLING.

Sell. Oh, dear Sir, what shall we do now? I have read that Benniger such a lecture, and taken the money *ad depositum*. But, good heaven! that fellow is a wild ferocious beast. He says, it is a bargain; that the receiver is the thief, and not the bidder. He insists on having the patent for the monopoly dispatched; if not, he swears he will play the deuce.

Reiss. So much the better; let him do his best.

Sell. Ah, but, dear Sir, he does not say a word against the Privy Counsellor; you and I are the scape-goats; every nerve trembles.

Reiss. So you are quite alarmed?

Sell. Truly.

Reiss. The rogue intended to bribe, and of course is liable to a heavy punishment.

Sell. But then he is a stranger.

Reiss. Have him arrested, then he can do no harm.

Sell. But he can talk a good deal for all that.

Reiss. That is my business. Have him arrested.

Sell. But the Prime Minister—

Reiss. Is at a great distance, and do not you know, though I do not publicly affect it, that I am the prime minister of this country.   Arrest him, I say.

Sell. Very well.   But then I have—

Reiss. What else? To the point!

Sell. A concern, that lies very near my heart.   I am told the Privy Counsellor is to resign,—and perhaps to leave this town.   I could not help making his sister considerable presents this morning, which cost a great deal of money; and, if his power should be at an end, all would be thrown away; he ought to re-imburse me.

Reiss. But those presents have been return-ed, I understand.

Sell. Without the least injury! but my ex-pence was heavy.   I must lose by those things, if I were to dispose of them.   Could not you manage so by your authority, that he should take them at prime cost?

Reiss. No, I employ my authority to better purposes.

Sell. Good heaven! the gown of rose satin alone cost me—

Reiss. (displeased.) Let it be converted into a morning-gown for yourself.

Sell. A morning-gown!—Ay, that will do. Rose colour becomes my complexion.   I thank you, it shall.   I will have it lined with lawn.   I will have it made up directly. *(Going.)*

Reiss. And have the fellow secured.

Sell. Directly! the morning-gown made up, and the fellow arrested!   I thank you for extri-cating me out of this embarrassment.   [*Exit.*

Reiss. Blockhead!—My whole existence is at stake;—once won, won for ever!

SCENE III.

Enter Sophia.

Soph. Father, I beg—

Reiss. Yes, you will soon beg.—Begone, be gone!

Soph. Your situation is dreadful, as dreadful as mine. Be kind and just. Lend your helping hand.

Reiss. Be gone to the Carpenter. Out of my sight, be gone, I say!

Soph. I am come,—I cannot leave you till your mind is at ease.

Reiss. I shall be at ease as soon as you depart, the spy of my actions. Be gone, I tell you!

Soph. Father!

Reiss. Begone, I tell you; begone, or I will have thee driven out of my house! Out of my sight, snake, serpent, traitor, spy, begone!

Soph. I have ever obeyed you, and I will even obey this cruel command. [*Exit.*

SCENE IV.

Enter Lawyer Wellenberg.

Well. You have sent for me;—here I am.

Reiss. I thank you;—sit down.

Well. What is your pleasure?

Reiss. I want to have a little conversation in a fair way.

Well. Propose fair things, and our conversation shall be fair. I will listen.

Reiss. Well, Doctor Kannenfeld is no more.

Well. It has pleased the Disposer of all Events to call him.

Reiss. Very fortunately for him! That slanderer, I would—

Well. Not so. Slanderer, not so,—a true penitent, a sinner, and of course one that has found mercy in the Divine Presence. He is dead as to his earthly frame, but the tears of repentance which he so often shed on my breast, I trust, will raise up fruits of joy and consolation in it: With respect to you, he is not dead as long as I live. To the point then; —in the name of heaven, what do you want?

Reiss. To offer a few propositions.

Well. Let us hear them.

Reiss. Sit down here, if you please.—*(Wellenberg sits down at the table.)*—Our good ancient German ancestors used always to drink a glass when they sat down on some good purpose, or when they had a mind to lay down some good rules for their descendents. *(Fills a glass.)*

Well. Ay, if there were any such good purposes in the present case, I would have no objection.

Reiss. Drink to a good intention, *(raising the glass,)* dear Mr. Wellenberg.

Well. When the good shall be atchieved, we will take a little wine; a very little, as an offering to gratitude.

Reiss. Wine cheers the heart of man.

Well. Good actions will cheer it much better. Come, *ad rem.*

Reiss. I am now possessed of the legacy,—you see. (*drinks.*) Your health.

Well. To your amendment.

Reiss. Very well, I thank you. (*Reaches him a glass.*)

Well. (*takes a sip.*) In the name of goodness.—

Reiss. I have resolved to do something for all that for the children, for whom I am very sorry.

Well. Something handsome. You must do every thing for the sake of the children and your own soul.

Reiss. What do you mean by that?

Well. You must give up the whole.

Reiss. You are not in earnest?

Well. Do you never expect to be called to an account for your actions in this world?

Reiss. The doctor's insanity has infected you.

Well. But the solemn oath, which I mean to have administered to you in a public court of justice, will open doors that you little expect.

Reiss. I can take it! the—(*Wellenberg rises.*)—Where are you going?

Well. Away! for—for—I am seized with a tremor at the mere idea that an oath does not shake your frame to its centre. What, will you stretch out your hand against the judgments of God? Methinks I see the very sparks of hell before my eyes; methinks I see an infernal fiend between you and me, writhing, hissing, and sneering; methinks I see him anxious to seize on your poor soul, as his prey for ever. I am ill; do good for once, and permit me to go home and throw myself on my bed. *(Going.)*

Reiss. Stay.

Well. I cannot.

Reiss. But, as the advocate of the children, you ought to hear my proposition.

Well. Then propose, briefly and fairly.

Reiss. Sit down.

Well. I must sit down; for the idea of your perjury has enfeebled me so, that I cannot move. *(Sits down.)* Propose to the honour of your Creator and the salvation of your soul, that I may recover my strength.

Reiss. Not as an obligation, but, through mere motives of pity and christian charity, I will give the children half of the legacy. What do you say to that?

Well. Half a virtue is no virtue at all; yet it is better than vice.

Reiss. Well?

Well. The fiend may yet lose his hold.

Reiss. Drink a glass.

Well. I almost stand in want of it, for I do not feel well on your account. *(Drinks off the glass of wine.)*

Reiss. What am I about! I have, in the warmth of conversation, left the bottle uncorked, and the spirit of the liquor, intended to honour you, will evaporate. No matter; *(takes the bottle to himself, and substitutes the other, out of which he immediately fills him a glass;)* here is fresh wine.

Well. (puts down the glass.) I will drink no more.

Reiss. But, when we have done and agreed, in token of reconciliation—

Well. My first and last words are, give up the whole of the bequest, or take the oath!

Reiss. Ay! what is all that!—(*Fills a glass for himself out of the bottle which he had removed from Wellenberg's side.)* A glass of wine will warm you. Come, touch here! (*Offers to touch glasses with him.*)

Well. No! the inclinations which wine inspires are false. Good inclinations ought to come from the heart instead of the bottle.

Reiss. Shall I tell you what carries me so far? It is your honest character, and my respect for you; and, as my daughter is a good-for-nothing hussy, I will, in the name of God, provided they let me alone while I live, I will, after my death, bequeath the remainder of the bequest to the children by a formal testament, which I wish you to draw up immediately. That is, upon my word, more than fair! Come, touch glasses upon that, and then we have done. (*Touches glasses with him, and drinks it off.*)

Well. (touches glasses, but does not drink.) That is something.

Reiss. Is it not! (*Fills his own glass.*) Well, then, off with it!

N

Well. (*holds up his glass, but does not drink.*) The good spirit begins to move you; and I begin to feel better in your company.

Reiss. (*wipes his forehead.*) I am glad of it.

Well. You wipe your forehead?

Reiss. Hem! you have put me in such a heat.

Well. Thank God! I wish you would examine your conscience fully, and then wipe your eyes too; then I would, in the joy of my heart, empty my glass at once.

Reiss. I thank you. Now to a prosperous futurity! (*Holds up the glass.*)

Well. In heaven,—yes! (*going to drink*;) but (*puts the glass down*) then every thing ought to be in a good state upon earth. Drink no more, it will heat you; and, to do good, the soul ought to be sober.

Reiss. Well then—

Well. In your proposition there may still be an acceptable compromise for the children. But—

Reiss. I should think so. Then accept it, give me your hand, and empty your glass.

Well. Ay, if it concerned only the children, I would accept it. But it concerns your soul, which cannot go out of this world in peace, if your conscience is not at peace. Therefore I do not accede to the proposition.

Reiss. What?

Well. I cannot accept it for the sake of your immortal soul, till you quite clear yourself, and give up the whole.

Reiss. Is that your last determination?

Well. It is.

Reiss. Then I will give up nothing at all.

Well. Then God have mercy upon you! I have done my duty.

Reiss. Does not the will itself secure me against every claim?

Well. Not quite so.

Reiss. I beg your pardon; does not Article V. say—

Well. If you avail yourself of that plea, and the good spirit has forsaken you, what must be the awful result! Think in time; what, to barter everlasting happiness for a few pieces of yellow dirt! Now I have done. (*Rises.*)

Reiss. The fifth article says, " that if ever"— Stop a little; I have the will at hand. *(Goes into the closet.)*

Well. I see there is nothing to be done here. God have mercy upon this obstinate man!— Has he not even tried to tempt me with his wine, that I might do what is evil? But heaven be praised, he did not succeed; and how easily might he have succeeded, though my nerves are worn out with age and infirmities! Besides, it is a very strong wine; *(takes the glass, and smells to it.)* Very strong! (*looks at it*;) rather feculent. (*Puts the glass down, walks a few steps, and seems to muse.)* Hem! (*examines Reissman's glass.)* This one is fine; (*looks again at his own glass*;) this is not so. (*Puts it down.*) This glass came out of the second bottle. He has not drank of that, I think. No,

he has not, I now recollect. Perhaps,—but
that is very wicked,—perhaps not content with
intoxication, he thought to get me to do the evil
that is in his soul? Such men are not to be
trusted; their notions are abominable. Perhaps
he mixed some intoxicating ingredient in this
wine? He is capable of such an action; for,
otherwise, why should he press me to drink?
Then my soul would have perished at the
same time with my philosophy!—I must know
that; I will have it examined; and, if so, I will
thank God for my deliverance, and withdraw
my hand for ever from the obdurate sinner.
(*Takes both bottles, and goes away with them.
When he has left the room, Reissman comes out of
the closet with the will.*)

Reiss. Look you here; here it expressly says.—
Where is he? (*Looks out of the door, comes back,
claps his hands together; pours the wine that is in
the two glasses out of the window; puts them in
his pocket; goes once more to the door, at which
the Lawyer went out. He is in a violent agitation; wipes the table very carefully with his
handkerchief; carries it into the closet, out of
which he returns with his hat and cane, and is
going out by the door towards the street. When
he is at the door he returns, carefully examines
the chair on which the Lawyer has been seated,
passes his handkerchief over it, carries both chairs
into the closet, examines the floor where the chairs
stood, and precipitately exit.*)

SCENE V.

Master Clarenbach's house.

MASTER CLARENBACH, SOPHIA.

Clar. Step in here, child! here you are, if not rich, at least safe. You have now done your duty as a daughter. Now recommend the perverse man to heaven, and let things take their course.

Soph. Can I be easy with that? It is lamentable, that I have no other means left.

Clar. My son has acted as a man of honour ought. He would not leave me till I had given him my word, neither to act nor to speak against your father.

Soph. You have given it.

Clar. And will keep it.

Soph. I will acknowledge it with filial affection, with the same care and attention as if I were your own daughter.

Clar. Jack has obtained you by noble means, dear daughter; that is a good and laudable commencement of the marriage-state.

SCENE VI.

Enter GERNAU.

Gern. Dear old man, I have forgotten all the wrongs the Privy Counsellor ever did me. They now vanish like a dream. He has more than compensated for all.

Soph. With respect to you?

Gern. That is out of his power now. But he has acted with such discretion, with such abun-

dance of good nature, and rendered so much justice to every body else, that I must be devoid of
all feeling, if I could consider my accounts with
him as unsettled.

Clar. Pray speak more of that. I have
been unwilling this long while to enquire
into the actions of my son; but to-day I am so
pleased with him, that I could talk of him for
ever without interruption.

Gern. He desired me to go home with him.
Away with every penny, said he, which I have
not acquired fairly, or of which the least doubt
remains. Then he counted money, sealed it up,
and called out to me repair to the next trading
town. I will give you the directions into whose
hands this cash is to go. I will wrong no man,
assist me to discharge my duty, name not who
sent it! I will set off this very day.—He is
this moment gone to pay two people, that had
been overcharged in their contributions towards the construction of the bridge. He in-
tends to discharge that debt personally, because
they are good people on whom he can rely, who
will not take advantage of his frankness.

Clar. Your work, dear daughter! a clear conscience, joy, and honour! what a valuable por-
tion you bring into my family! When at even-
ings we shall meet, and every one of us shall
sum up the honest earnings of the day, with
what affection and gratitude shall we then cal-
culate and pay you the interest of your capital!

SCENE VII.

Enter FREDERICA.

Fred. Your father has been here this minute to enquire after Lawyer Wellenberg.

Soph. (*quick.*) Is he gone yet?

Fred. He seemed in doubt some time, whether to go or stay, but then he went without saying any thing.

Clar. Ah, the legacy,—his conscience,—Dr. Kannenfeld,—it begins to operate.

Gern. Yes, yes.

Soph. Oh, I wish that was settled!

Clar. Do not be uneasy; old Wellenberg has him entirely in his power, and he knows what he is about.

SCENE VIII.

Enter Privy Counsellor CLARENBACH.

P. Coun. Sophia, I have kept my word.

Clar. (*reaches him his hand.*) We have been told so.

Soph. I know it.

P. Coun. My accounts are now settled, and my mind is at ease. I can now call a furnished house and four thousand dollars · my own honest property. I have thrown off the burden, I have got rid of a connection that imposed upon me.

Gern. Dear brother! how is it possible that any connection should warp your generous principles.

P. Coun. Man does not warp all at once, but by degrees. Providence lent me a hand. (*Lays Sophia's hand on his breast.*) You even look kinder than you used to do.

Fred. I should never have forgiven you, if you had compelled me to give my hand to Selling.

P. Coun. Dear Frederica!

Clar. Well, well! that was done while he was intoxicated with foreign wine. The cup of pride produces that,—a good and useful beverage for those that quaff it in moderation. Whoever cannot do that, had better drink home-made wine.

Soph. But what do you intend to do with regard to your office, and the charge brought against you concerning the monopoly?

P. Coun. I mean to set off for the capital, and candidly lay the whole before the Minister; he is a good man; I will tell him I assumed a burthen too heavy for my shoulders, and entreat him to lay it on some person better suited to bear it.

Clar. That is right, Jack! When I was desired to sketch a design for the Prince's palace in our neighbourhood, I also said, "Please your Highness, I am a carpenter; the undertaking is beyond my sphere; send for an architect, and what he plans I will endeavour to execute. My head may conceive the plan for a common dwelling-house well enough, but not for a palace; and so I do not wish to step out of my line." The old Prince has since repeatedly thanked me for it, and said, with a significant nod, " You were right, master, Clarenbach! I wish some of my counsellors would do the same, and, when called on, say, I am not fit to fill that office. But they take the hatchet in hand, and slash away without any art or judgment."—My dear son, throw it down, and let some good political carpenter take it up. God be with you!

SCENE IX.

Enter Lawyer WELLENBERG.

Well. Are you all here?—thank God!

Clar. You are welcome, Mr. Wellenberg.

Well. A chair, a chair. (*P. Counsellor reaches a chair.*)

Clar. What is the matter with you, pray?

Well. O Heaven! oh!

Fred. What ails you, Sir?

Gern. You make me uneasy.

Soph. Have you spoken with my father?

Well. Yes, yes, yes.

P. Coun. Dear Wellenberg, pray speak plain.

Well. Est necesse, ut remotis testibus loquar.

P. Coun. Dicam ergo aliis ut abeant.

Well. Imo, jubeas, quæso! sunt enim res summi momenti.

P. Coun. Nunquid sane de sponsæ meæ parente?

Well. Quin ita! agitur enim vitæ et animæ salus.

P. Coun. Good folks, leave me a minute alone with this good gentleman.

Clar. Good God!

Soph. It concerns my father.—O Clarenbach!

P. Coun. We will manage all for the best.

Soph. To your compassion, to your filial compassion,—to your duty as a son, to your heart, to every thing I appeal, Clarenbach! You must bring him back to the path of virtue, even against his will. You must, and my gratitude shall be eternal.

SCENE X.

Enter Aulic Counsellor REISSMAN.

Reiss. Mr. Wellenberg!—

Well. Oh, that God—(*Rises.*)

Reiss. I want to speak with you.

Well. No, no! I will not.—Keep off, keep at six yards distance from me at least.

Reiss. I must have a private conversation with you.

Well. God forbid!

Soph. Dear Mr. Wellenberg grant it; I entreat you.

Well. Can I?—ask him.

P. Coun. I beg, I entreat you.

Well. (*after a pause.*) Well, yes. Yes then, I will run the risk.

Soph. I thank you.

Well. But—(*beckons the Privy Counsellor to come near him, and whispers to him.*)

P. Coun. Yes, I will. Come along.

Reiss. (*alarmed.*) What,—what, will you?

P. Coun. Nothing that can give you any uneasiness.

Reiss. Where do you intend to go?

P. Coun. To win this hand and your esteem. Come along. (*All exeunt, except Reissman and Wellenberg.*)

SCENE XI.

Aulic Counsellor REISSMAN, *Lawyer* WEL-LENBERG.

Reiss. Ay, dear Mr. Wellenberg, you are— it is—why are you—I cannot conceive for what reason you left my house in that abrupt manner.

Well. The warning came from above to the unworthy. (*Takes the bottle out of his pocket.*) What is this? (*putting it on the chair.*) Answer me that!

Reiss. How!—(*snatching at it.*)

Well. Keep off!—It is poison!

Reiss. Ay, good God!

Well. There is poison in the wine you pressed me to drink.

Reiss. Should you by some unfortunate mistake—

Well. It is poison! it was intended to close my lips for ever! Lulled to sleep by your artful proposals, I might have passed into the other world according to the old proverb, " Dead men tell no tales;" but you forgot that I should rise against you at the last day.

Reiss. (*assuming courage.*) Mr. Lawyer, dare you—

Well. I dare call you an assassin.

Reiss. Who knows what you have been doing with this bottle in the mean while?

Well. So you think to escape by your cunning? This moment I see, and you feel, the mark which the Almighty has impressed on your brow. Your mind is callous, and yet you are so struck with terror, that your tongue cleaves to the roof of your mouth, and cannot perform its office.

Reiss. But, you, you—

Well. Silence! Is your soul insensible to the trepidation of your body, or what I have not in my power to do? Here stands the evidence of the crime, there the delinquent, and here I stand, either as judge or a merciful man, if you deliver yourself up vanquished into my hands; and, if not, as your accuser before the tribunal of the public. Kneel down this moment, the sword of justice hangs over your head!

Reiss. (*shaking.*) My God!

Well. You are at the end of your career! The judgment of heaven is committed to my hands, but mercy reigns in my heart: act in such a manner, that my heart may preponderate; for I am a man whom you have driven to extremes.

Reiss. (*with terror.*) What, what must I?—

Well. To the extreme, I say. I can hardly refrain from demanding justice.

Reiss. What is your demand then?

Well. For myself I demand nothing. But what does your conscience demand, wicked man? Is it silent? (*With warmth;*) Then, then I must do what I ought to do.

Reiss. Well, then, I will give up the legacy at once.

Well. Further—

Reiss. What can I do more?

Well. Resign your office, that the corroding canker may be removed from the breast of my country.

Reiss. But—

Well. God and man demand that I should utter this language.

Reiss. I will, I will.

Well. Consent to the Privy Counsellor's marriage, and do not disinherit your virtuous daughter. All these points must be reduced to writing, and signed by you this very day; then I will remain silent, and spare you, that mercy in turn may be shewn to me.

Reiss. I will. Let the seal of silence be placed for ever on your lips.

Well. For ever!

Reiss. Give me your word and hand.

Well. My word is sufficient. (*Puts the bottle in his pocket.*) If you accomplish the conditions, this affair shall be buried in eternal oblivion.

Reiss. All shall be done this very day.

Well. Now go, and inform the people of all the blessings you intend to shower on them.

Reiss. I will grant them every thing, but I cannot tell them the happy effects of our conversation.

Well. It must be so to save appearances.

Reiss. You are right! (*Takes a ring from his finger.*) Accept this, it is of the first water, worth two hundred Louis d'ors.

Well. The tears of joy that your virtuous daughter will shed are the purest christian water, and sparkle better. Those I will accept, and thank God for the tribulations, for by this he has enabled me to purchase what is good. Now go. I wish you to die well and soon. Thus I discharge the sinner from his terrors and my hands, and recommend him to the hand of the Father of all.—(*Reissman slaps his forehead, and exit.*)—I think I have done well; at least, I do not know how I could have done better. He has stood before the executioner; if that do not shake and convert him, his good angel will veil his face and fly from him, and then he will soon be hurled whither I would not wish.

SCENE XII.

Enter Master CLARENBACH.

Clar. Old friend, you have performed wonders!

Well. Not I, not I, (*looking up to heaven,*) but another.

Clar. He restores the legacy to the poor orphans; he consents to my son's marriage.

Well. Even so, he has done no more than the duty of a Christian.

Clar. He does not disinherit his daughter; he gives the children their inheritance.

SCENE XIII.

Enter Privy Counsellor CLARENBACH, SO-
PHIA, FREDERICA, *and* GERNAU.

P. Coun. Matchless man!

Soph. Eternal, eternal gratitude!

Well. (*Puts his hands in his pockets.*) Spare my weak hands; my heart is sound!—

P. Coun. How was it possible, how did it happen?

Gern. Tell us.

Fred. I cannot conceive it.

Well. That—

P. Coun. He uttered all these benefactions in such a hurry—

Fred. And at the same time looked nobody in the face—

Gern. And then he ran away.

Clar. I never saw a man do so much good in so ungracious a manner.

Soph. Good God! but he has done it after all, and—

Clar. Well, well; but how did it come about?

Well. Never ask that question again!—never! Do you understand me?

Clar. We thank God it is so; why should we enquire how it came to be so?

Well. That is right, friend Clarenbach! (*To the Privy Counsellor.*) And you resign the Privy Counsellorship?

P. Coun. My abilities are not adequate to it.

Well. Have I not told you a hundred times, when he was what they call a Lawyer, and when he wrote with such humane feelings, with such fire, with such indefatigability, in the cause of justice, — Master Clarenbach, said I, Jack stands very high on level ground; do not suffer him to rise higher, for he will tumble down.

Clar. It is true upon my word.

Well. So you came down of your accord? that is well done!

P. Coun. Henceforth I hope to prove useful to mankind. Under your guidance, I will be a Lawyer once more.

Well. (*with a smile.*) Lawyer! I cannot bear that name; it conveys the idea of an entangled net, or of a deceitful guide, that will lead you out of the way into the pathless desert. We should not be called Lawyers, but the Friends of Justice.

Clar. Yes, yes; Friends of Justice, the foes of chicanery!

Well. Who will not plead in an unjust cause! Do you promise that? Have you the resolution to be an honest Lawyer?

P. Coun. With the greatest pleasure.

Well. Write little; act a good deal; take little money; have a good stock of honesty and kind intentions; apply but seldom for advice to the *corpus juris,* but often to the heart; and to the hour of death I shall esteem you. I shall lead the way by the course of nature, but it will yet be a consolation to me in my last moments to think I have left an honest man behind me,—a man that will wipe away the tears of the widow and the orphan.

Clar. Jack, listen to the words of this good old man; let them sink deep into your heart; let them be your model! He possesses little worldly wealth; but, at the last day, what myriads that now roll in wealth would wish that they had possessed as little and done half as much good with it; but it is not for me to judge; I only say, make him your model.

P. Coun. Dear father, I will.

Enter Aulic Counsellor REISSMAN.

Reiss. I am come to tell you what I know will please you. How sweet are the tears of repentance! how refreshing to the drooping soul! I have at last settled my accounts with my conscience; I owe much, but I will endeavour to pay all. Now I feel in earnest that I am a father, and this is my dear daughter! (*Embraces Sophia.*)

Soph. O my dear father, the serenity of your brow, like a mild evening-sun, sooths the perturbation of my mind. I see that all is peace within. This single moment of joy would repay an age of sorrow.

Reiss. O my child! (*embraces her again;*) and this is my son! (*embraces Privy Counsellor; Clarenbach takes him by the hand.*) I am now completely happy, my mind tells me so; my feeble sight was dazzled with the false lustre of gold; but honest Wellenberg took me by the hand

P

and conducted me into the path in which I ought to walk in the evening of life.

Clar. I have not wept for some time; but nature, on the present occasion, has indulged me with a few tears, and they shall be paid on sight. (*takes Reissman by the hand.*) We are both in the evening of life; let us descend with even step to the grave; our dear friend Wellenberg will be our guide. Let us leave our children behind us, and, if any evil should tempt them in an unguarded moment, may our example interpose like a guardian angel! Splendor and ambition are gaudy signs, painted by the hand of delusion, to lead the bewildered traveller still farther astray. (*Gernau kisses Sophia's hand, and gazes on Frederica with fond attention.*)

Soph. (*embraces Frederica, and drops a tear.*) Excuse me, I have a tear for joy as well as sorrow.

Clar. Come, let us not delay the nuptial rites.   [*Exeunt omnes.*

THE END.

W. WEST, No. 27, PATERNOSTER-ROW.

The BEAUTIES of the late Right Honorable EDMUND BURKE, felected from his Writings, &c. alphabetically arranged, including feveral celebrated POLITICAL CHARACTERS, drawn by himfelf, and his own Character by different Hands. To which is prefixed a SKETCH of the LIFE, with many original ANECDOTES of Mr. BURKE. In two Volumes, 8vo. Price 10s. Boards.

" This work contains many original anecdotes which efcaped the notice of Mr. M'Cormick and Dr. Biffet, and which, relating to Mr. Burke's private life, are peculiarly interefting.

" With regard to the fpecific merits of the compilement, as a felection, we may obferve, that the extracts from the multifarious writings of Mr. Burke, appear to be judicioufly felected, and the general mafs feems to be very properly reduced to order."—*Monthly Review for December*, 1798.

ST. PIERRE's celebrated STUDIES of NATURE, carefully abridged, with a copious INDEX, by L. T. REDE, in one handfome Volume, 8vo. Price 6s. Boards.

This work is peculiarly adapted to infpire, in the breaft of youth, the higheft reverence and profound adoration for the wifdom and benevolence of God in the works of the creation, which the Author has difplayed in fuch fine language, that it cannot fail to form the tafte for compofition, at the fame time that it improves the head and expands the underftanding.

The BALNEA, or a HISTORY of all the popular WATERING PLACES in ENGLAND, in 12mo. By GEORGE SAVILLE CAREY. the fecond Edition, Price 3s. 6d. in coloured Paper.

" Carey, at whofe eccentric entertainment we have laughed many an hour, has here produced a moft pleafant and lively *mélange*, the refult of much whim and obfervation, blended with a vaft fund of genuine anecdotes, and a very particular account of the various amufements, cuftoms, manners, and inhabitants of the places of fafhionable refort in this kingdom."—*Monthly Mirror for January*, 1799.

ANECDOTES and BIOGRAPHY, including many modern Characters in the circles of fafhionable and official Life, By L. T. REDE, 8vo. Price 7s. Boards.

" This is almoft without exception the beft collection of anecdotes ever perufed. The Editor difcovers good tafte, both in his choice of materials, and the various occafions in which he prefents himfelf to his readers, and fpeaks in perfon. We acknowledge ourfelves indebted to his induftry, for a fund of very agreeable entertainment," &c. &c.— *New London Review for January*, 1799.

The ELEMENTS of CHEMISTRY, tranflated from the German of JOSEPH FRANCIS JACQUIN. Price 7s. 6d. Boards.

PETER PINDAR's TALES of the HOY, interfperfed with Song, Ode, and Dialogue, 4to. Price 3s.

The NATURAL and POLITICAL HISTORY of the STATE of VERMONT, one of the United States of America; wherein is difcovered the primary Caufe of the late American War, &c. &c. by IRA ALLEN, Efq. Major-General of the Militia of the State of Vermont, with a coloured Map, 8vo. Price 6s. Boards.

www.ingramcontent.com/pod-product-compliance
Lightning Source LLC
Chambersburg PA
CBHW032145010726
47493CB00008BA/2580